PHOENIX PRECINCT

PHOENIX PRECINCT

Keith R.A. DeCandido

eBooks
Pennsville, NJ

PUBLISHED BY
eSpec Books LLC
Danielle McPhail, Publisher
PO Box 242,
Pennsville, New Jersey 08070
www.especbooks.com

ISBN: 978-1-956463-17-0
ISBN (ebook): 978-1-956463-16-3

Interior Design: Danielle McPhail, McP Digital Graphics
Cover Design: Mike McPhail, McP Digital Graphics
Current Design based on previous cover design by Jenn Reese
www.tigerbrightstudios.com
Phoenix Medallion © Mike McPhail,
    based on the style of Yakutsenya Marina

Art Credits - www.fotolia.com
Medieval sword © michelaubryphoto

*Dedicated to folks who seek out a better life,
even if they don't get what they bargained for.*

ACKNOWLEDGMENTS

THANKS AS EVER TO THE TRIUMVIRATE OF MAGNIFICENCE THAT IS eSPEC BOOKS: Danielle Ackley-McPhail, Mike McPhail, and Greg Schauer. Thanks also to my mighty agent Lucienne Diver, who does what she does so very well.

Thanks to my wonderful editors Wrenn Simms and GraceAnne Andreassi DeCandido, who keep my prose from getting excessive and wrong—and yes, they are, respectively, my wife and my mother, but they're also professional editors of many years' experience. It pays to marry well and have the right family, folks...

Thanks to John Ordover, the editor who not only bought *Dragon Precinct* for Simon & Schuster back in 2004, but suggested the title, which pulled the whole series into focus. Thanks to the folks at Dark Quest Books who rescued the series in 2011 after S&S discontinued the imprint that *Dragon Precinct* was part of, and Elektra Hammond, who served as editor of the four novels that were originally published by DQB. Thanks to the aforementioned Danielle Ackley-McPhail, Randee Dawn, Rosemary Edghill, the late great C.J. Henderson, Lee Hillman, L. Jagi Lamplighter, Jeffrey Lyman, Jonathan Maberry, Jean Rabe, Jennifer Ross, Patrick Thomas, and Michael A. Ventrella, who have all commissioned short fiction in this universe. And thanks to all the Kickstarter, Indie GoGo, and Patreon supporters who made several of the short works and vignettes I've done in this universe possible.

Thanks to ToniAnn Marini, Kyle McCraw, Matthew Holcombe, Meredith Peruzzi, Sas Nelson, Anneliese Hopwood, David Mack, and most especially the Forebearance for everything. And eternal gratitude to the furry things: Kaylee and Louie here at home, and our supplemental fuzzballs, Professor Zoom, Tempura, Jazz, Loki, Thor, Eden, Jax, Hima, and Spot.

Finally, thanks to our good and noble Kickstarter supporters! (A list of which appears at the back of the book.) You are all the very very best humans. And elves. And dwarves. And gnomes. And halflings.

PROLOGUE

TUCHERA HAD NEVER BEEN SO EXHAUSTED IN HIS LIFE. OR SO HAPPY.

For months, he'd been trying to find landscaping work. Back home in Barlin—before the fire, obviously—he'd had his own landscaping company with fifteen employees. The nobility of the city-state—most of whom lived in the hilly region of Timnor Heights—were always after him to fix up their gardens and the make the outside of their mansions look anywhere from presentable to fabulous. Tuchera had gained a strong reputation for giving clients what they asked for and also, most importantly, for sticking to his estimates.

Then came the fire.

Like so many of his fellow Barlin natives, Tuchera had been forced to move his family away. Both their home and their business were so much ash and smoking dust now. Tuchera's oldest son, Mairo, was killed. His wife, poor beautiful Migda, had a perpetual cough that could only be ameliorated by healing potions they could no longer afford.

In Barlin, Tuchera had owned a large house in the middle-class district of Barlin. All three kids had their own rooms, and Migda had a craft room where she could sew her tapestries. Now, Tuchera, Migda, and their remaining children, the twins Hamno and Voro, were crammed into a single room in the Albinton region of Cliff's End. Tuchera had found odd jobs here and there, but nothing in his actual skill set. Migda's continuing cough made it impossible for her to work, and the twins were still too young to earn a living at anything. Tuchera had made barely enough to feed, clothe, and house them in their tiny living space.

Which was why he had been so grateful for Gedling.

Gedling lived in the small house next door to Tuchera and his family. He was also a landscaper, and he'd been working a job in Cliff's

End's upper-class district, remodeling the garden of the Fansarri mansion. Tuchera was envious of the work, and Gedling had admitted that he'd been lucky to get the job. He'd even offered to see if Tuchera could be added to the crew, but there were no positions open.

Tuchera hadn't even been sure he *wanted* that. He had *run* a landscaping company, and a part of him had felt that being one of the menial workers doing landscaping was beneath him.

It was Migda who pointed out to him that the work he *was* doing was even more beneath him than that. He'd been loading crates on the docks, delivering packages in the middle-class neighborhoods, running errands for the taverns in the lower-class sections of the city-state. Once, he even did some cleanup work in Jayka Park, which he could almost convince himself was similar to landscaping.

So when Gedling came home from work one day saying he wasn't feeling well, and could Tuchera take his shift for the next two days? Tuchera instantly said yes.

The hardest part the first day was not trying to manage the land-scaping. The Fansarris had their notion of how they wanted their lawn and garden to look very precisely worked out. In Tuchera's professional opinion, the master landscaper — a very tall human named Fulban — was showing very little imagination.

However, by the day's end, he had had brief encounters with both Sir Boslin and Lady Elmira, and then he understood. He'd had clients like these two. The lack of imagination shown by Fulban was a direct result of the very explicit instructions given to him by the Fansarris.

At the beginning of the second day, Fulban approached Tuchera. "You did very well yesterday. If I'm honest, you're better at this than Gedling."

"Thank you, sir." He hesitated, then decided to throw in all his coins, as it were. "I actually ran a landscaping business in Barlin."

Fulban frowned down at him. "What's your name again?"

"Tuchera."

"I know your work! I travelled to Barlin for a family wedding two years ago. You did the Zerbenig Atrium, yes?"

Thrilled to be recognized, and even more thrilled that Fulban had seen the atrium in question, he proudly said, "Yes, that was me."

"That was stellar." Fulban's face then fell. "You got caught in the fire, I take it?"

Tuchera just nodded.

"I think I can justify adding you to the payroll, so you can keep coming back after Gedling gets better. I can't guarantee you anything more than what you're doing as a laborer, but—"

"That's fine," Tuchera said quickly.

By the time he finished the second day, he was exhausted. He was in better physical shape now than he had been back in Barlin, particularly with all the manual labor he'd been doing. But those other jobs had been an hour or two at a time, not an entire day's worth of physical activity, and after two days of it, he was wiped out.

But still, he had an actual job in his actual field! Despite his exhaustion, he walked happily down Meerka Way and turned onto Boulder Pass, which would bring him to Albinton.

The neighborhood had been created specifically to handle the influx of refugees from Barlin following the fire. Lots of people called it "New Barlin" for that reason, which Tuchera had always found to be silly. That wasn't the name of the section, Albinton was, after the recently deceased lord of the demesne.

He had mentioned this to Migda, who had smiled at him and asked, "Where are you doing this landscaping job again?"

"On Shade Way."

"No, I mean what part of Cliff's End are you working in?"

"The upper-class district."

"You mean Unicorn Precinct?"

Tuchera had let out a sigh. "That's a ridiculous name. I mean, I suppose the Castle Guard uses it, but that doesn't mean the rest of us have to."

"But that's the name of the region," Migda had said, pointing out the absurdity of his complaint about "New Barlin."

He'd said nothing in response, and she had another coughing fit, and then they talked about other things.

From what he'd been told, the part of Boulder Pass that intersected with Albin Way—the latter being the road that encircled Albinton—had been a dead end, right at the large boulder for which the thoroughfare was named. Boulder Pass had been reorganized to go around the boulder instead of ending at it, and then intersected with Albin Way.

Previously, the other side of the boulder was the Forest of Nimvale, but a large portion of it had been cleared out by the order of Lord Doval and his mother Lady Meerka, and Albinton built in its stead.

Tonight, as he reached that intersection by the boulder, four people in hobgoblin masks approached him, blocking his way forward. They stood side-by-side on Boulder Pass. One was shorter than the others — probably either a gnome or halfling, he wasn't bulky enough to be a dwarf — while the other three were likely human, though the masks covered their faces and ears, so one or more could've been an elf. While real hobgoblins had orange fur and yellow faces, these masks were in different colors.

"Goin' home, *bahrlan*?" That was the tallest of them, his voice muffled by the red hobgoblin face that covered his own.

Tuchera closed his eyes and sighed. Bahrlan was a word in Ra-Telvish, the elven tongue, meaning "filthy," but it sounded enough like "Barlin" that it had become a common slur directed toward Tuchera and his fellow refugees over the past few months.

"Please, I don't want any trouble."

"Too bad, 'cause we do," said the very short one, whose mask was green.

Red mask yelled, "Answer the question, *bahrlan*, you goin' home?"

"I just finished a very long day of work, and — "

"Work?" Another one of them stepped forward, the only one whose mask was the proper yellow color. "How come *you* get to work?"

"Excuse me?" Tuchera asked, confused.

"I'm from right here in Cliff's End. Born and bred. And I can't find work. How come *you* can find work, you stupid little *bahrlan*?"

The last one, whose mask was orange, muttered, "Probably workin' for shit wages."

"Yeah," yellow mask said, "taking work away from the rest of us."

"I'm being paid the same as any landscaper," Tuchera said defensively. In fact, one of the things he most liked about Fulban was that he paid comparable wages to what he himself had paid his workers back in Barlin.

That seemed to get all four of their backs up. Red mask stepped forward and raises his arms, hands clenched into fists.

"Did you say landscaper, *bahrlan*?"

Tuchera swallowed. "Y-yes. For — for the Fansarri family."

And then, without another word, red mask reached back and punched Tuchera right in the stomach.

All of a sudden, Tuchera found that he couldn't breathe. He doubled over, pain shooting through his entire torso as he struggled to inhale properly.

Then yellow mask kicked him in the shin, causing him to fall to the ground, and then his entire world became a haze of pain and breathlessness as fists and feet collided with every part of his body over and over and over again.

Dimly, he was able to recognize when they stopped, but their ceasing to punch and kick him did nothing to ameliorate the pain.

Tuchera heard voices, but he wasn't sure which was which, especially since they were all muffled.

"Now that we finally got him, can we go home now?"

"C'mon, there's gotta be more *bahrlans* we can beat up."

"Not with his body laying there. Someone'll be by soon."

"I *know* someone'll be by soon, that's my point! It's another *bahrlan* we can—"

"We can't be here when they find this guy's body! Pay attention, will you? Besides, we got our money."

"I agree, let's go."

"Fine."

Their footfalls moved away. Tuchera couldn't tell if they were walking into Albinton or back down Boulder Pass. Not that Albinton was likely, since it was full of what they called *bahrlans*…

He could no longer feel his legs. Or his arms. Or much of anything else, either. He stared up at the star-filled sky, but found that his vision was also fading.

A voice that seemed infinitely far away was now speaking. "Are you all right, sir?"

"Look at 'im, 'e ain't even close t'all right."

"Try to find a healer."

"Yeah."

"Can you tell me who did this, sir? Sir?"

Tuchera tried desperately to answer the question, but he couldn't make his mouth work.

His last thought before darkness claimed him was of Migda and the twins.

ONE

CAPTAIN DRU ENTERED THE LORD AND LADY'S DINING ROOM TRYING NOT TO salivate over the smell of the sausages.

A month and a half ago, Lord Doval had invited Dru to breakfast to discuss some issues with the Cliff's End Castle Guard's reports. By the end of the meeting, Doval had suggested they do this at the end of every week.

The part of Dru that was the head of the Castle Guard was a bit iffy about that, but the part of Dru that enjoyed a good meal thought it was a brilliant idea. The castle chef made the best sausages Dru had ever had, and no matter what else was served for breakfast — wheatcakes, fried potatoes, fruit compotes, various omelettes — after seeing Dru's response to the sausages, the chef had always made sure to include a plate of them on the side for the captain.

And the meetings themselves had been fruitful. Both Doval and Dru had only been in their jobs for a bit over a year now. Doval had inherited it from his brother Blayk, whose reign lasted barely a month. It had been cut short by the revelation — from Dru and his fellow detectives in the Castle Guard — that Blayk had had his and Doval's father Lord Albin killed and had also tried to kill King Marcus and Queen Marta. Attempted regicide was a capital crime, and with Blayk's demise, Doval took over, running the city-state of Cliff's End with his mother, Lady Meerka.

As for Dru's new position, Blayk had done a major shakeup of the Castle Guard, including encouraging Captain Osric — who'd run the Castle Guard for a dozen years — to retire. Blayk's hand-picked replacement was the incompetent Amilar Grovis, who very sensibly chose to step down after Blayk's arrest. Dru — whose heart hadn't been in being out on the thoroughfares of Cliff's End pursuing criminals ever since his partner Hawk had been killed during a bank robbery — got the job.

As Dru sat down to his breakfast — the chef had done a pepper-filled omelette today — Lord Doval regarded him quizzically. "I'm starting to think that your neglecting to shave is not simply an attempt to emulate your predecessor, Captain Osric."

Dru laughed as he speared a sausage link with his fork. "Nah, I decided to grow a beard. Torin shaved his, so I'm fillin' the gap." Osric always seemed to have perpetual stubble but never grew a beard and was rarely clean-shaven. Dru had never understood how his erstwhile boss managed it…

Doval chuckled. "I see. Lieutenant ban Wyvald's recent tonsorial alteration is a bit off-putting, I must admit. I can understand your growing your beard in protest."

"It was my wife's idea," Dru said after swallowing some egg and pepper, "after she saw Torin's new look for the first time." He recalled with amusement the look of horror on Zan's face when she saw Torin ban Wyvald — who had had long red hair and a thick red beard for longer than either Dru or Zan had known him — with short hair and a thin goatée.

After taking a sip of his tea, Doval got down to business. "I've noticed a bit of an uptick in crimes in Mermaid Precinct."

"Yeah, I noticed that, too," Dru said. "I'll talk to Sergeant Mannit, but I'm thinkin' it's mainly 'cause the dock extension ain't finished yet. The docks're more crowded than ever, 'cause'a all the construction workers, but there's the same amount'a space, 'cause they can't use the extension for nothin' else. And it's been goin' on for months now. How close are they to finishin', anyhow?"

"The guilds have informed me that the work should be completed next month." Doval smiled wryly. "Though they told me that last month, as well. The guilds have been in a bit of disarray since the Gorvangin Rampages. Though I'm led to understand that the guild leaders who were arrested are due to be released soon?"

Dru nodded. "When the barge drops off prisoners next month — not this month's batch, that's later this week, but next month's — all the guild leaders who were part'a that'll be free."

"I'm hoping the guilds will be less — realcitrant? After that." Doval popped a bit of omelette into his mouth to punctuate the point.

For his part, Dru refrained from comment. The guilds had been trying to unite, and the so-called Gorvangin Rampages—intended to show their displeasure with being refused in that desire—wound up making things worse. The guilds' leadership were all imprisoned, and their replacements were either surly, incompetent, or both. It had led to a lot of issues with getting work done around the city-state, especially the dock extension.

Getting those leaders back might serve to make things better, but Dru wasn't optimistic. He suspected that only time would accomplish that. But he also knew, after a year of working with him, that his lordship did *not* want to hear that, so he kept his peace and ate some more sausage.

"The good news is that crimes in N—" He coughed. "In Albinton have dropped considerably." He knew that Lord Doval hated the "New Barlin" nickname. "Phoenix is doing its job."

"That is good to see, though I'm not sure how you come by that. It seems to me that the amount of crime in Phoenix Precinct is equivalent to the reduction in same in Dragon and Goblin Precincts."

"It's actually less. Not by much, but it is less. And the crimes we are seein' are at the extremes, which you always see: the petty shit and the big shit. Pocket-picking, disturbing the peace, that kinda stuff, and the big things like murders are about the same, but the middle stuff—which is way more dangerous than the little things and way more common than the big things—is down."

"Interesting." Doval sighed. "I wish there was a way to reduce the—" He smiled. "—petty shit and big shit."

"Right there with you, m'lord, *believe* me." Dru ate the last bit of sausage, happy to be eating it, but sad that it was the last one. "In fact, I complained about that after I got promoted to detective a few years back. Me an' my old partner, Hawk, we kept havin' to deal with this guy, Jerri Donoh. We'd both dealt with his people when we were guards, and now that we were detectives, we figured maybe we could nail 'im for real on somethin'. But we never could. After we tried to arrest him one time, Osric told me somethin' I always try to remember."

"And what words of wisdom did the former general have for you, Captain?"

"He said that the whole point of the Castle Guard ain't to stop crime, it's to mitigate it. People are gonna be people. That means that they think they can get away with the petty shit 'cause it's petty, and they do the big shit 'cause it's big, and whatever reason they have for killin' someone or beatin' someone up, it's more important to the people doin' it than anythin' else. But if people know we're here, it may stop them from doin' it, and if they do do it, at least we're here to get justice for their victims."

Doval nodded thoughtfully. "A wise man, Captain Osric. Though it's too bad that such mendicants as this Donoh person are able to function with impunity."

"Mostly, yeah. But he *does* function with impunity at least in part 'cause people need him for the petty shit. That's what it all comes back to, like Osric said."

"Indeed. I wonder if Blayk was wise to force Osric to retire."

"Oh, he wasn't," Dru said quickly; one thing he had learned over the last year was that Doval had no issue with hearing his late brother spoken poorly of. "He was *way* better at this job than I am. But he wouldn't'a stood for all'a crazy stuff your brother tried to do."

"Definitely not."

Finishing off his omelette, Dru realized that he was running out of time to discuss something in particular that he wanted to talk to Lord Doval about. "There's one more thing before I get to work, m'lord."

"This isn't work?" Doval asked.

"Oh, yeah, it is, but it's also pleasure, thanks to your chef." Dru grinned cheekily. "I don't get breakfast at home, an' Sergeant Jonas's wife's pastries are good, but nothin' like this."

Doval frowned. "Why don't you get breakfast at home? Do neither you nor your wife cook?"

"Oh, Zan cooks, but she's makin' breakfast for the kids."

"I wasn't aware that you had children."

"We don't." Dru chuckled. "Didn't I ever tell you what my wife does?"

"Apparently not," Doval said. "Or if you did, I'm sorry to say that I don't recall."

Dru couldn't recall if he'd ever told his lordship, either. "Zan cares for a bunch of kids during the day. The mornings're spent gettin' ready for the kids, so she ain't got time to make me breakfast, and I ain't got the talent to do it. And sometimes we get kids stayin' with us overnight for a while, so she's gotta get them ready, too."

"I see. Well, that explains why you so readily agreed to these meetings."

In fact, Dru had been very reluctant to agree to these meetings six weeks ago, but knew it was impolitic to say that out loud. "Anyhow, there's one more thing to talk about, if you don't mind, m'lord."

"Of course."

"There's one type of assault we're seein' way more of, an' that's people targeting refugees from Barlin."

Doval let out a sigh. "Still?"

Dru nodded. "It went down a little when Phoenix opened, but it's back in force. They ain't doin' it *in* Albinton as much, at least, but in Dragon, Mermaid, an' especially Goblin, we're seein' way more of it, especially on the night shift."

"That is distressing. Though I believe your Captain Osric's beliefs about the nature of people apply here. Still, we should do *something*, I think. Perhaps a curfew? That will keep the streets emptier at night, and reduce the possibility of such assaults."

"I don't think that's such a great idea, m'lord." Dru had actually considered suggesting it, and talked it over with Sergeant Jonas and all six of his detectives yesterday, and they'd collectively come to the conclusion he was about to present to Doval. "The guards'll all be too busy enforcing the curfew, an' the types'a people who'd do this wouldn't give a shit about a curfew anyhow. In fact, they'll prob'ly find it easier to beat people up, 'cause they'll be able to attack folks when they're comin' home to make curfew. Plus, it'll piss off a lotta people."

"I suppose. Still, we should do *something*."

"Well, it might help to get a couple more detectives. The six I got're stretched pretty thin right now. The OT helps," he added quickly—he'd been fighting for more overtime for a while now, and finally got it last week, "but two more detectives'd make it easier to close more cases and put more of the bad guys in the hole instead of out doin' crimes we can't stop 'cause there's a bunch more people livin' here."

"We did do a recruitment drive after the fire," Doval said, as if Dru didn't know that.

"Yeah, that was for guards, and that's been great. But we need more detectives for—" He sighed. "—for the big shit."

Doval rubbed his chin.

It took a great deal of work, but Dru somehow managed to not break into a triumphant grin. Over the last thirteen months or so, the captain had come to recognize a lot of his lordship's tics and tells. One such was that, when he rubbed his chin like that, he'd decided on a course of action, but wasn't entirely sold on it and would come up with one final excuse to not do it.

"I'd have to talk my mother into it—she controls the budget, after all."

Dru was ready for that. "Lady Meerka is a big fan of both Danthres and Torin, especially after your brother. I can send them over."

With a snort, Doval said, "Oh, I'm aware of Mother's admiration for Lieutenant Tresyllione in particular." Torin's half-elf partner Danthres Tresyllione first, Dru knew, came to Meerka's attention after that business with the female mage, whose very existence put the Brotherhood of Wizards' collective noses out of joint. "Very well, if she approves it—and feel free to have the lieutenants plead that particular case—then it will be done."

Dru grinned under his beard. "Thank you, m'lord. Seriously, this is huge."

"Don't thank me yet, as it hasn't actually *happened*."

"Yeah, but you're considering it, which puts me ahead of three months ago, when you *weren't* considering it."

Doval chuckled. "Well said, Captain. I believe that's all, yes?"

Taking the hint, Dru got to his feet. "Yeah. Till next week, m'lord?"

"Indeed."

With that, Dru retreated through the tapestry-covered corridors of the castle to the eastern wing and the Castle Guard squadroom.

The view of the Forest of Nimvale from the picture window that took up the entire north wall of the squadroom never failed to impress Dru. It was even more lovely than the view in the dining room.

Only three of the people who worked directly under him were present: Sergeant Jonas, who was shuffling scrolls about; the elven Aleta lothLathna, Dru's former partner, and once a member of the Shranlaseth, the Elf Queen's elite enforcement squad; and Dannee Ocly, the half-dwarf, half-human who was the most recent addition to the squad, and who'd proven to be quite good at the job despite her overall pleasant, optimistic demeanor. After a couple of months on the job, she had yet to show the veneer of cynicism that every other detective Dru had known grew to acquire, if they hadn't had it already when they joined up. The latter two were going over the paperwork on the Lowerre case.

Manfred and Kellan, he knew were supposed to testify before the magistrate this morning. To Jonas, he asked, "Where are Torin and Danthres?"

"Danthres is on a call at Boulder Pass. Torin's late, as usual. I sent one of the youth squad to fetch Torin at home and send him to join her."

Rolling his eyes at Torin's perpetual tardiness, Dru asked, "What's the call?"

"A Barlin refugee was found dead right by the boulder."

Dru looked to the ceiling in supplication. "I was just talkin' with his lordship about that."

"Did he suggest a curfew?" Jonas asked.

Nodding, Dru said, "I told him why we all thought it was a bad idea."

"We *all* didn't," Jonas said bitterly. He'd been the only holdout even after they'd discussed it for an hour.

"Almost all," Dru said with a smile.

Waving his arms, Jonas said, "It's fine. I'm just grateful you asked for our input. Osric only asked for my help when he wasn't able to come to a decision. You ask all the time."

"Yeah, well, I lost track'a the number'a times Hawk and I bitched that the captain didn't consult us on somethin', and we both always swore that if either of us got promoted, we'd check with the rest of the squad on stuff."

Grinning, Jonas said, "Glad you didn't forget that when you got promoted, sir. Not true of most folks."

Dru nodded in gratitude. "Who's the refugee who got killed?"

"Not sure. Someone from the youth squad came in and said some *bahrlan* was beaten to death. And *yes*," he added quickly, "I declined to give the boy a copper tip until he apologized for using that word and swore he wouldn't use it again. Personally, I wouldn't bet any more coins on him keeping to that promise."

"Me either, but from now on, they don't get the tip if they use that word, I don't care if they apologize." Dru couldn't do much to curtail people's bigotry, but he could, at least, do that.

He had to do *something*…

TWO

Torin ban Wyvald woke up to an empty bed.

He sighed, running his hand through his short red hair. He and Jak
Reesh had been in a relationship for several months now, and Torin had
thought that it was deepening.

But for the third straight night, Jak had promised that he would
come sleep in Torin's home after his late-night job, and he didn't.

Sighing a second time, he clambered out of bed and splashed some
water on his face from the basin. The time chimes had rung six, and he
needed to get to the castle.

As he performed his morning ablutions, he mused on the fact that
he very rarely reported for work on time. Indeed, the number of times
over his eleven years in the Cliff's End Castle Guard in which he made
it to the squadroom at or before seven could be counted on the fingers
of both hands.

But he'd been early for his shift each of the last two days because he
couldn't bear to be in his apartment without Jak in it.

Not that they actually lived together. And since he'd started his
late-night carpentry job, the ritual had been that Jak would arrive
some time in the middle of the night and curl up into Torin's bed with
him. Torin would wake up some time in the morning and just watch
Jak sleep.

Without a sleeping Jak there to observe, however, Torin didn't want
to be in the apartment any more than necessary.

Had Jak not promised to come to his home that night, it would've
been one thing. It was the dashed expectation that saddened Torin.

Still, at least Jak was working. The carpenter had been struggling to
find employment for all the time that Torin had known him. It was odd
for there to be an overnight carpentry job, but Torin in truth knew very

little about how that trade worked in Cliff's End. In any case, it was good that Jak had a job, at least, even if it was denying them their opportunities to spend time together.

As Torin was putting his leather armor on, a knock came at the door.

Walking over to the door in his bare feet, he opened it to reveal a blonde-haired girl from the youth squad—one of the many poor and/or ne'er-do-well children who ran errands for the Castle Guard—who smiled up at him. "Hiya Loot ban Wyvald!"

Torin smiled down at the girl, whose name, he finally recalled through his not-quite-awake-yet haze, was Daith. She had trouble with the word "lieutenant," and refused to be so crass as to call him by his given name, so she used the prefix "Loot" for all the detectives. "What can I do for you, Daith?"

"Sargeant Jonas said to come getcha! Got a dead body on Boulder Pass. Loot Tresyllione's already on her way."

"Where on Boulder Pass?" Torin asked.

"Right by the boulder! Hey, didja know why that boulder's there?"

Smiling indulgently, Torin gave a response that was both the truth and a lie: "I've no idea why the boulder is there."

"Well, I can tell ya! See, there was this great hero from *years* back, name'a Kall. Big strong guy, he was, and he was here in Cliff's End fightin' a dragon, y'see, and he threw a big rock at him! It missed, though, and it landed here, and then the dragon breathed on him and he died. Couldn't nobody move the big rock after that, so it just stayed there."

"Fascinating." Torin moved back into his apartment and grabbed his money-pouch, which was still attached to the belt he hadn't yet put on. Liberating a copper piece from same, he tossed it at Daith. "Thank you for that story—and for fetching me. I need to finish getting dressed, but I'll head directly to Boulder Pass."

Daith caught the copper unerringly. "Thank *you*, Loot!"

After Daith ran off, Torin finished up, putting on his belt, his boots, and his earth-colored cloak. Both armor and cloak were emblazoned with the gryphon design that indicated that Torin worked out of Gryphon Precinct, which was the formal name for the castle that was the city-state's seat of government. The cloak itself symbolized his rank of lieutenant, making him one of the Castle Guard's detectives, charged with solving the more complex crimes committed in the demesne.

Including, sadly, murder.

He exited his apartment and worked his way first over to Meerka Way—the main thoroughfare of Cliff's End, which went from the castle all the way to the docks—then turning right at Boulder Pass to head toward New Barlin.

He arrived at the boulder that gave the thoroughfare its name to find his partner Danthres Tresyllione already present, along with several guards wearing armor decorated with a phoenix crest, symbolizing the recently opened Phoenix Precinct.

His tall, half-elf, half-human partner spied his approach, broke into a huge grin, and turned to one of the guards. "You owe me a silver, Jared."

"Shit!" Jared shook his head. "Thought I had that one."

Holding out a hand palm-up, Danthres said, "Well?"

Looking guiltily from side to side, Jared quickly said, "I ain't got it on me right now—but I'm good for it! Catch me at the Chain tonight!"

"If you're not there, I'll find out where you live." Danthres's tone was only mock-threatening, but Jared swallowed nervously nonetheless. Torin's partner could be very intimidating, even when she wasn't trying to be...

Raising an eyebrow as he approached Danthres, Torin asked, "Dare I ask what the wager was?"

"That you'd get here before Boneen."

Throwing up his hands, Jared said to Torin, "You're late every damn day, Lieutenant, you couldn't be late today?"

Chuckling, Torin said, "My apologies, Jared." Regarding his partner, he asked, "You were obviously *very* sure I'd beat Boneen here, if you bet a silver."

"What I was betting was that Jak would've blown you off again, and you'd once again be out of the house faster than usual." Danthres's face—an unfortunate mix of her father's tapered ears, high forehead, and thin lips and her mother's wide nose, large brown eyes, and sallow cheekbones—grew more serious. "It would've been worth losing the silver to be wrong, though. Are you all right?"

"No, but I suspect what will cure my ills is a case to sink my proverbial teeth into. So what do we have?"

"Escalation." Danthres led Torin over to where the body of a human lay bloody and broken.

Torin sighed. "There've been, what, five assaults on Barlin refugees since Phoenix Precinct opened?"

"Five reported ones," Danthres said bitterly. "But this is the first murder."

"Do we know who this is?" Torin asked.

Jared said, "I've seen him around, but I don't know his name."

None of the other guards knew him, either.

"Dammit," Danthres said, "he's been here all night. *None* of you know him?"

Another guard, Simon, said, "I mean, I know his face, but damned if I know where he lives or nothin'."

Just then, Afrak, a diminutive human guard came onto the pass from New Barlin. "Yo, Salvit, Slaney wants you back at the precinct!"

Salvit sighed. "What's Sergeant Shitbrain want *this* time?"

With a snort, Afrak said, "You think he told *me*?" Then he looked over at the body. "Lord and lady, who killed Tuchera?"

Torin exchanged a glance with Danthres, then asked, "You know this man?"

Afrak nodded. "Yeah, he used to be a landscaper in Barlin. Got a family over on Central Way. Migda'll be crushed. She's sickly, can't work, and they've got a couple kids."

"Finally," Danthres muttered.

"No need to be snotty about it, Tresyllione," came a voice from behind Torin.

He turned to see a short wizard approach. This was the magickal examiner, Boneen, on loan from the Brotherhood of Wizards to aid the Castle Guard. The main way he did his job was through an Inanimate Residue Spell, or a "peel-back," which enabled him to determine what happened in a particular location.

"I wasn't referring to your arrival, Boneen," Danthres said, "though I'm grateful for it. I'd love a description of whoever killed this man."

"Then you'll have to leave."

"Of course," Torin said. He turned to Jared, and the other Phoenix Precinct guards. "Keep a perimeter that will allow Boneen to cast the spell and don't let anyone through." The peel-back only worked if there were no living beings in the range of the spell besides the caster.

"We know the drill, Lieutenant." Jared then grinned. "It's the rookies in the castle and Unicorn you gotta worry about."

"Indeed." Torin knew that Jared and the others were good at their jobs. He had to remind himself that, while the construction of Phoenix Precinct had been done after a major recruiting drive to add to the Castle Guard's ranks, Phoenix itself had been staffed by veterans. Jared, Afrak, Salvit, and the others were all transfers from Dragon, Goblin, and Mermaid, while the rookies were all assigned to lighter duties in Unicorn or Gryphon.

Turning to Afrak, Torin said, "Please, take us to Tuchera's residence?"

"Youbetcha, Lieutenant."

Salvit snarled. "Guess I'd better go with you, see what Sergeant Shitbrain needs."

"How long," Danthres asked slowly, "have you been referring to Slaney by that nickname, Salvit?"

Suddenly apprehensive, Salvit said, "Oh, no, ma'am, it's just a—I mean, it's—that is to say—"

Torin was unable to keep himself from giggling.

Holding up a hand, Danthres said, "No, it's fine! Slaney's a moron of the highest order. I've met senile trolls that would make better sergeants. I just want to know how long it's been going on, and who thought of it. That second part mostly so I can buy the person in question a drink."

"Danthres," Torin explained, "served with Slaney in Goblin back in the day."

"And he was an even bigger shitbrain then," Danthres added.

Afrak made a noise like a bursting pipe. "That ain't possible."

"You have my deepest sympathies, Lieutenant," Salvit said. "I've only been serving with him a few months, and I'm figuring he's got blackmail material on Lord Doval or something."

"No," Torin said, "he simply saved the life of Ferro Winit."

"Son," Danthres added, "of Sir and Madam Winit, the construction ministers."

"Figures," Afrak muttered.

As they walked into New Barlin itself, initially walking on Albin Way, which ran around the periphery of the neighborhood, Torin decided to change the subject, as any discussion of Sergeant Rik Slaney tended to sour Danthres's mood. "I heard a new boulder story today."

Danthres rolled her eyes. "Lord and lady, not again!"

Torin laughed.

"What's she on about?" Afrak asked.

Throwing up her hands, Danthres said, "Go ahead and tell him, or I will."

Grinning widely, Torin said, "About two years after I joined the Castle Guard, Danthres and I caught a case at the boulder. Much like today, it was a dead body, though that one was placed after being murdered elsewhere. I asked why the boulder was there. Danthres told me the story she was told — that it was the cornerstone of the original castle that served as the seat of Cliff's End."

"Well, that's nonsense, that is," Afrak said. "Everyone knows that the boulder was put there by Helsek Gam when he banished the dragonriders."

Salvit looked at his colleague with irritation. "The dragonriders are the ones who banished Helsek Gam, not the other way 'round! Anyhow, that's not the truth — the boulder's really all that's left of the great beast Matahooq after he was turned to stone by Hwang."

"And now you see my joy," Torin said enthusiastically.

"And my agony," Danthres said in a low moan.

"I've collected dozens of different stories about the boulder — in fact, I've heard that Helsek Gam put it there, that the dragonriders put it there, and that it was Matahooq many times. Though some of the latter said instead that it was all that was left of one of the dragons who banished Helsek Gam, turned to stone by that wizard, rather than Matahooq."

They got to the intersection of Albin Way and Central Way — the latter bisected the neighborhood — and before Danthres, Torin, and Afrak could turn off down that road, Salvit, who had to continue on Albin Way, said, "Wait, before you go — what's the story you heard, Lieutenant?"

Torin smiled, and shared Daith's tale of Kall's losing fight against a dragon.

"Why does everyone insist there be a dragon in the story? It was one of the great beasts, it's obvious." Salvit sighed. "Best go see what Sergeant Shitbrain wants."

Danthres smiled. "I will *never* tire of that nickname."

THREE

Up until this morning, Jora Kenspal had considered herself to be one of the luckier ones.

"Luckier" in this case was a relative term, given that she, like so many others, lost her home when the fire raged through Barlin. But they'd had some warning, as the fire had already started, but not yet spread to the Kenspal home. They were able to gather their belongings — and, more importantly, Jora's crafting supplies — before abandoning their home.

Forced to relocate to Cliff's End, Jora had convinced her wife Edda and their daughter Lyis to try to rent space in Jorbin's Way, a thoroughfare devoted entirely to mercantile commerce in the middle-class region known as Dragon Precinct. Edda's job as a bank manager was not one she could re-create in Cliff's End — there was only one major bank, plus a few smaller ones, and they all *had* managers for their branches, and didn't even have job openings at the lower levels.

Jora's craftwork had always been a fun sideline, something to make a little extra money. Lyis had even started helping, as she had an aptitude for crocheting, freeing Jora to do the more complex sewing and beadwork for the higher-ticket items.

But now, it was their best way to try to make a living in their new home.

Fortunately for them, one of the merchants on Jorbin's was retiring and was looking for someone to sell his space to. In fact, he specifically wanted to give his space to a Barlin refugee, as he'd lost family to the fire.

And so within a few weeks, the Kenspals were making decent money. People loved her work, Lyis was getting better and better at crocheting—her colorful blankets in particular were quite popular—and Edda was an excellent salesperson.

At this point, they had saved up enough to be able to consider renting an apartment close to Jorbin's instead of the tiny room they all had to share in New Barlin.

But then came this morning.

Their stall had been vandalized, their merchandise torn and ripped and unsellable.

They had summoned a guard, who then summoned two detectives from the castle.

Another way in which the Kenspals had been lucky was not having had to deal with the Castle Guard in any meaningful fashion. Sure, some guards were there to make sure the crowds moved in an orderly manner when they arrived at Cliff's End and patrolled the area outside the city-state where the refugees were staying while New Barlin was being finished, then they kept an eye on things as they moved in.

But the only direct interaction any of the Kenspals had had with any guards before today were the few who'd stopped by the stall to buy Jora's clothes. In particular, one older guard with a green cloak—which, she later learned, meant he was a sergeant—bought one of Lyis's blankets, saying it was for his wife. A week later he came back and said it was her favorite blanket, as it was the only thing that kept her warm *and* comfortable when it got cold at night.

She had rather hoped that streak would continue, but alas.

The two detectives—who wore brown cloaks—were an elven woman and what looked like a human woman mixed with a dwarven man. The elven woman had a hard face, and moved confidently; she seemed to be looking at everything at once. The other woman was much more relaxed and friendly. Had this been another circumstance, she wouldn't have even considered trying to sell anything to the elf, but her partner was someone she suspected would be amenable to nice clothes and pillows and blankets and such.

Not that she'd be selling either of them, or anyone else, anything for a while.

"I'm Lieutenant Aleta lothLathna," the elven woman said. "This is my partner, Lieutenant Dannee Ocly. Can you tell us what happened?"

"Not in any detail I'm afraid, Lieutenant. I'm Jora Kenspal, I run this stall with my wife and daughter."

"Where are they?" lothLathna asked in an almost accusatory voice.

Trying not to sound resentful, Jora said, "Lyis, our daughter, was *very* upset. I sent her home with Edda."

Ocly quickly asked, "How old is Lyis?"

"Ten. She does the crocheting."

Putting a hand to her hairy chin, Ocly said, "Oh, that must be so rough on her. I'm so sorry. That was probably the right idea."

After being put on the defensive by lothLathna, Jora appreciated Ocly's genuine-seeming apology. "Thank you."

"We will need to talk to Lyis, and to your wife, at some point," Ocly said, "but not right away."

"I understand," Jora lied. She didn't see what they would tell them that Jora herself wouldn't, as they all came to the stall at the same time.

"If you could tell us what you can," lothLathna said, "in whatever level of detail you can provide."

Nodding, Jora said, "The three of us came to open the stall this morning, and found it like this." She indicated the stall with her left hand.

Both lothLathna and Ocly turned to gaze more closely upon the broken stall. The tables were splintered, the legs on one of them shattered. Piles of clothes were scattered about the ground.

"I assume you lock the merchandise away overnight?"

Again, Jora nodded. "The lockboxes were smashed to pieces." Then she smiled grimly. "The amusing part is, the locks themselves are still intact." She went over to the one table that was still in more or less decent shape, where she'd put the two padlocks that went on the boxes. She picked them out and held them out to lothLathna.

The elf peered at them and shook her head. "It seems they were quite determined."

"I know."

"Is there anyone who you know of who might have targeted you?"

Jora shrugged. "Not that I can think of. All our customers have been satisfied. Honestly, Lieutenant, we've only been here a few months, since we came from Barlin."

Ocly brightened at that. "You're from Barlin as well?"

"Yes. We lost our home in the fire, and came here. Did you as well?" Jora wouldn't have thought the fire was long enough ago for someone to come here, join the Castle Guard, and become a lieutenant.

"Not the fire, no, I moved here five years ago."

I'm glad you came willingly, at least, Jora thought bitterly, but thought better of saying aloud. That wasn't fair to the lieutenant. Instead, she continued with her point. "We haven't been here long enough to make enemies."

"No irate customers?"

"Some, I suppose, but not so much so that they'd do *this*."

"Have you been harassed due to being from Barlin since arriving here?"

Jora looked away nervously. "We, uh—we don't advertise that we're from Barlin."

That put an annoyed look on Ocly's face. "That's ridiculous."

"But necessary," Jora said firmly. "We've all seen what's been happening to far too many refugees. On our way here, we saw that one was killed. Lyis was already upset about that, which is another reason why I sent her home with Edda."

"Two of our colleagues are on that case," Ocly said.

"There's no one else who's bothered you?" lothLathna asked.

Jora sighed. "Just a few Ghandurha worshippers when they saw Edda and I holding hands. We got that from those types in Barlin, as well—their god apparently objects to any union that isn't a man and a woman. They get upset when they see a woman with a woman"

"Or a human with a dwarf," Ocly said with a nod. Jora assumed that she, as a halfbreed, and her parents had received similar opprobrium from Ghandurhans.

"But they're also nonviolent, in my experience," Jora added. "They gave us dirty looks, but that was it. They'd never do something like this." She sighed. "It's just so frustrating. We make our payments!"

"Payments?" lothLathna asked.

"Both of them, yes. We bought this stall from a merchant named Henly who was retiring. We're paying him in installments. Plus, the protection tax, of course."

That seemed to bring both detectives up short. "Excuse me?" lothLathna asked.

"The protection tax."

"You have to pay a protection tax?" Ocly asked, aghast. "I can't believe the nobles would force that on you!"

"Oh, no, it's not the nobles. At least, I don't think it is. No, it's the security force that keeps an eye on the Way at night. I honestly don't see what good it does to pay it if they can't even keep *this* from happening."

LothLathna turned to face the guard who'd initially come over, who was still lingering nearby. "Garis, do you know anything about this?"

"Nope. But I'm still kinda figuring my way around, y'know?" At Jora's questioning expression, Garis added, "I just transferred from Unicorn Precinct, ma'am."

"Who do you pay?" lothLathna then asked Jora.

"Every week, someone comes by with a box that has a gold ankh on it. That's the logo for the security force. I've seen a few people walking around with that same ankh emblazoned on their clothes. It looks rather gaudy, and I've been thinking about offering to make them nicer tunics with the symbol." She sighed. "But that won't be happening now. It'll take *days* for us to make new stock. I don't know if we'll even be able to make our payments, never mind find a new place to live."

"I'm sorry about that." As with before, Ocly sounded sincere.

"We're going to have the M.E. come by to do a peel-back," loth-Lathna said.

Jora frowned. "I didn't understand most of what you just said."

"Sorry," lothLathna said, and for her part, she was *almost* sincere sounding, "a wizard who casts a spell that allows us to find out what happened in a particular locale. It should help us identify the vandals."

Garis said, "His mage-bird came by before you arrived, ma'am, said he'd come here after going to Boulder Pass."

Both detectives winced at that. Ocly said, "We may not get him to do it, then."

Jora's face fell. "Why not?"

"Boneen gets tired very easily." LothLathna's words were bitter indeed. "Or so he says. Getting him to two crime scenes in one day is sometimes a challenge. And unfortunately a murder is higher priority than vandalizing."

That led Jora to ask another question. "Why are detectives handling this? I mean, I'm grateful, but—wouldn't someone like him," she pointed at Garis, "be tasked with this?"

Ocly said, "Normally, yes, but our captain wishes us to crack down on vandalism, plus Garis here is hardly the only new transfer. A lot of people have changed precincts of late since we opened Phoenix Precinct, and they're still getting the hang of the new beats."

"Besides," lothLathna said, "this security force is not sanctioned by the Castle Guard, and will *also* need to be investigated…"

On the one hand, Jora thought lothLathna was being a bit unfair. After all, the Castle Guard couldn't be everywhere, and apparently they were struggling to keep up with things.

On the other hand, it's not as if the security force in question actually did their job to stop whoever vandalized Jora's stall...

FOUR

THIS, DANTHRES THOUGHT, *IS REALLY TURNING INTO A WRETCHED DAY.*

Starting with a dead body was always a bad start. On the one hand, Danthres joined the Castle Guard at least in part to make sure that murderers (and other criminals, but mostly murderers) saw justice for their crimes. On the other hand, she would've been much happier if her job wasn't necessary.

That dead body being yet another Barlin refugee victimized by members of Cliff's End imbecile contingent—a fairly large club, to Danthres's eternal annoyance—made it even worse. The violence against the refugees was getting worse.

And then there was her winning the bet with Jared, which just meant that Torin and Jak were still having problems. She hated seeing her partner unhappy, partly because it happened so rarely that when he was miserable, it brought the entire universe down. Torin's optimism and cheeriness was one of the few good things in the world that Danthres could count on, and to not have it was nigh devastating.

That was followed by one of the least pleasant tasks in her job: death notifications. Telling someone that their loved one was never coming home was a critical part of all the detectives' jobs, and also the most emotionally wrenching.

Tuchera's wife Migda handled it better than most—probably because, as refugees from the disaster in Barlin, she was pretty well used to life defecating in her soup—but her twin children began wailing and crying and shouting and screaming.

Once Migda calmed them down, they were, at least, able to get *some* useful information out of the widow.

"No, Tuchera got along with everyone. He went out of his way to be friendly to people. And it paid off—one of our neighbors took sick and offered Tuchera his shift."

"Doing what?" Torin asked.

"Landscaping." Migda closed her eyes, tears welling up in them. "For Wiate's sake, he'd been looking for something in his field since we came to this sewer of a city-state, and he finally found it, and *this* happens."

Danthres said, "The guard who identified him said he owned a landscaping company back in Barlin?"

Migda nodded. "We didn't have the capital to start over here, unfortunately. The bank was claimed by the fire and we lost all our savings *and* the company's money. This would've been such a great opportunity for him." She started to weep. "Dammit."

"We're so sorry." Torin was always the one who said that, as he was better at sounding sincere. Danthres was also sincere when she said it, but she never *sounded* that way, so she usually left such condolences to her partner.

Migda then started coughing, a fit that lasted several awkward seconds. "My apologies," she said, once she got it under control. "My parting gift from Barlin. I've had this cough since the fire, and we haven't been able to afford any of the decent remedies."

They took more information, including the name of the neighbor, Gedling, who gave him his shift, the name of the Cliff's End landscaper he was working for, and also what Migda wanted them to do with the body. Were they back in Barlin, Migda would have wanted a funeral and burial, but they couldn't afford either, so she told the detectives to simply have the body burned.

After they left Migda to her grief, Danthres and Torin went to the house next door, where Gedling lived. Danthres asked Torin about the Fansarris, for whom Tuchera had been working, "We're going to have to—to *talk* to those nobles, aren't we?"

"It is extremely likely, yes," Torin said dryly as he knocked on Gedling's front door.

After several seconds, there was no answer. Danthres peered in the window, which had a sheer curtain that prevented one from making out details of what was happening inside, but still allowed for detecting motion. "I'm not seeing any signs of life in there."

"We'll have someone from Phoenix check back."

Danthres winced. "That means we have to *go* there and talk to Slaney."

"We have to do that in any case, as we need to know about other assaults."

With a sigh, Danthres said, "I suppose." This just added to the overall wretchedness of the day. She'd despised Rik Slaney from the second they'd walked a beat together in Goblin when she was a rookie and he left her to subdue a troll all by herself, and he'd done everything he could in the dozen-plus years since to work his way down from that estimation.

Working their way back to Albin Way, they arrived at Phoenix Precinct. With a start, Danthres realized she hadn't been to the precinct itself since she was present for the opening ceremony a couple of months ago. Unlike Dragon, Goblin, and Mermaid Precincts, Phoenix wasn't a converted military barracks, or a converted mansion like Unicorn Precinct, but rather a building specifically built for the purpose of being a Castle Guard precinct house.

For one thing, it had a proper set of doors instead of the ridiculous swinging doors that were favored by barracks. It was also more of an open space, with the sergeant's desk in the center of a large room with dozens of desks. One flight down were the holding cells, collectively referred to as "the hole," as they were in most every precinct.

Sitting at that circular desk in the center of the big room was Slaney.

Expecting her conversation with the sergeant to be the low point of her wretched day, Danthres found herself cheered by the sight behind the circular desk: Slaney looked like he'd lost a great deal of weight, he hadn't shaved in days, and he had bags under very red eyes.

Torin sounded far more concerned than Danthres felt when he asked, as he approached the desk, "Are you all right, Sergeant?"

"The hell d'ya want, Lieutenants? Can'tcha see'm *busy*?"

"There's a witness we need to talk to on Central Way—Gedling, the next-door neighbor of our murder victim, Tuchera. He wasn't home, and we'll need guards to check there and send him to the castle when he's home."

"Yeah, fine, whatever, look, I got a lotta work t'do 'ere. This job's real complicated-like."

Danthres said, "Part of your job, Sergeant, is to do what your superiors tell you to do, and we both outrank you."

"Yeah, yeah, fine, Tresyllione, be a bitch like usual. Look, I got a tonna paperwork that's all backed up, I got people bein' beat up all'a time—"

"In fact," Torin said, "that is one of the things we need to know about. We need some details about the other incidents of Barlin refugees being assaulted."

"Yeah, that's kinda the paperwork that's backed up. Look, the magistrate's crawlin' up my arse, I gotta find six different reports that prob'ly ain't even done yet, so if'n y'don't mind, *Lieutenants*, us sergeants got *real* work t'do, all right?"

With that, Slaney stormed off and headed toward the staircase downstairs.

Shaking her head, Danthres said, "Why am I not surprised that that shitbrain can't actually handle this job?"

"Oi," said one of the guards, whom Danthres recognized her as Ebnig, one of the transfers from Dragon, "y'should speak with the respect 'e deserves. You should call him *Sergeant* Shitbrain."

Several of the other guards laughed at that, as did Danthres.

"Is he doing as terrible a job as it seems he is doing?" Torin asked Ebnig.

Snorting, Ebnig replied, "Nah—it's worse. Only reason the precinct's still runnin' right is 'cause'a Sergeant Kaplan."

Danthres nodded. Ander Kaplan was the sergeant in charge of the night shift. She asked, "Guard, do you know anything about the attacks on refugees?"

"Just that they're happenin'." Ebnig shrugged. "We keep tryin'a stop it, but it ain't easy. Folks is pissed, y'know?"

"How badly have the victims been hurt?"

"Oh, nothin' too terrible—till last night, anyhow. Jus' bruises and a broken bone'r two."

Torin scratched his bare cheek. "I wonder what was so special about Tuchera, then."

"Let's hope it *is* something special," Danthres said, "and not just that the attacks are escalating."

They left the new precinct and headed back to Boulder Pass, only to find Boneen with a sour expression on his face.

"Don't tell me," Danthres said as they approached, "the peel-back was blocked by some kind of stupid magick or other?"

One of the great frustrations of the Castle Guard's job—especially in the last few years—was criminals who found ways to block Boneen's peel-back. It was becoming increasingly common, and Danthres was getting well and truly sick of it.

"No, the peel-back functioned properly," Boneen said, "and it revealed that there were four assailants."

"That's good," Torin said.

"All four wore hobgoblin masks that covered their entire heads. One was sufficiently diminutive that he could've been a dwarf or gnome or halfling, but beyond that, I cannot tell you race, skin color, or any other manner of physical description, save for the fact that they had four different *colored* masks: red, green, yellow, and orange."

Danthres snarled. "That's not good."

"The masks," Boneen said, "were likely cheaper than a spell to block my peel-back would have been."

"No doubt," Torin said. "Thank you, Boneen."

"Can you make crystals with their images?" Danthres asked.

"What's the point?" Boneen testily queried.

"It'll show the clothes they were wearing, and perhaps someone might have seen the masks."

"Very well, if you insist, Tresyllione." With that, Boneen made several complex gestures. Danthres covered her sensitive eyes just as the wizard disappeared in a flash of light.

Jared was still hanging around, and Danthres said to him, "The family can't afford any kind of funeral, so send the body to the shop."

"Right," Jared said. He went off to fetch a detail of other guards to carry Tuchera's corpse to the body shop, a cave outside the city-state, where a dwarf named Orvag burned bodies that weren't claimed.

Torin regarded his partner. "So, we have a victim everybody liked attacked for no reason by four people we have no useful description of."

"Oh, there was a reason." Danthres sighed. "He was a *'bahrlan.'* Just many damned *idiots* in this city-state. Most of the population of Cliff's End wasn't born here—including four of the six detectives! Why single out these people, who didn't even come willingly?"

"You're asking for logic from bigots, Danthres," Torin said gravely. "In my comparatively reduced experience with bigotry compared to, say, yours, I have found that such is a waste of time. And you should be fully aware of that, given your own history."

Blowing out a breath, Danthres said, "I know, I know." Danthres was raised in Sorlin, a now-defunct colony to the south that catered to refugees, particularly people who had elven blood but were not pure-blood elves, and therefore in violation of the Elf Queen's purity laws. The defeat of the Elf Queen a dozen years earlier and the subsequent repeal of the purity laws had made things easier for halfbreeds like Danthres and other mixed-race folks, but the majority of elves still held Danthres in contempt because her mother was human.

"C'mon," Torin said, "let's get back to the castle and report to the captain."

Danthres blinked. "Hmp."

"What?"

"You called Dru 'the captain.'"

"He *is* the captain," Torin said slowly. "Has been for over a year now."

"I know, but—" Danthres chuckled. "I don't know, he's always been 'Dru' to both of us—back to when he was an idiot guard getting in the way of our cases. Osric was the captain."

"He was, but I believe that Dru has done an excellent job in the role and deserves respect." Torin grinned. "More, say, than Sergeant Shitbrain."

"*That's* for sure. And you're right, Dru has grown into a fine captain. I suppose it's just odd to think of him that way. Ah, well. Let's head back."

As they ambled down Boulder Pass, Torin said, "Since we must travel through Unicorn to get back to the castle, we should probably talk to the Fansarris on the way back."

Danthres sighed. She'd forgotten about Tuchera's temporary employer. "Fine, we may as well get *that* over with."

Definitely a wretched day...

FIVE

"Ten gold? For a *cigar*?"

Hobart sighed as he stared at the well-dressed elf that stood across his table on Jorbin's Way. "It's a *Barlin* cigar, isn't it? Since the fire, it's an easier job findin' yourself a vampire than a Barlin cigar."

"There aren't any more vampires." The elf had been holding his head up high so he could look down past his nose at Hobart, but now he was just staring confusedly.

"My point." Hobart sighed. "Look, I only got me five'a these stogies left. I seen 'em goin' for fifty gold here onna Way, not to mention what some *bahrlans* are askin'."

The elf scoffed and went back to raising his head up high. "Please. Some filthy mendicant on the docks claimed to be from Barlin and to have one of his people's cigars, and offered it to me for a hundred gold. Mind you, it was plain brown parchment wrapping oregano leaves…"

Hobart couldn't help but chuckle. "Yeah, well, you ain't gonna getcherself a fair deal from *nobody* onna docks. But me, I'm an honest merchant. Ask anybody here onna Way, I've been sellin' my wares here for twenty years now."

At that, the elf smiled. It wasn't a particularly pleasant smile, as it reminded Hobart of that you saw on a cat right before it chowed down on a mouse, and Hobart rather wish the elf had retained his previous haughty mien. "I came over here *despite* your reputation, Hobart, not because of it."

"Fine, if'n you know all about me, then y'know one thing for damn sure: I don't mess around when it comes t'cigars. I'm a connoisseur, I am. Hell, only cigars I even *smoke*'re Barlins."

"Then why would you sell any of your last five?"

"'Cause they're my last five, an' I ain't like t'get no more any time soon. I'm a connoisseur, like I said — an' I like to be sharin' with like-minded folk who're also connoisseurs. I'm assumin' that's you, or you wouldn't even be here." In fact, Hobart knew it was the case based on the light-colored residue on the elf's fingers. Cheap cigars left much darker markings on the fingers of those who smoked them. This was a gentleman who only smoked the good stuff, and his fancy clothes bespoke someone who could *afford* the good stuff.

The elf went back to looking down on Hobart, for which the merchant was grateful, as that smile was horrible. "I first went to Barlin six years ago. I was in a tavern there, and was sold a cigar by the barkeep. I'd had human-made cigars before, and they'd all been horrendous. I was very much looking forward to telling the barkeep precisely what was wrong with his cigar — and then I took a puff."

Hobart grinned knowingly. "Sounds familiar."

"I've never been able to stand smoking anything else since then. So yes, I've come to you, because since the fire, I've searched all over Flingaria for Barlin cigars, and haven't found any. I've found plenty of fakes — that one on the docks was merely the least convincing."

"Well, I'm tellin' ya, these ain't no fakes," Hobart said, "and they're my last five, so if you wanna buy one, it'll be ten gold. And I ain't budgin' from that."

"Ten gold for a two-silver cigar."

Hobart held out his hands, palms-up. "Supply an' demand. Ain't no supply, so it ups the demand. Look, you don't wanna, don't. I ain't gonna have no trouble findin' — "

"Fine!" The elf shouted that word to the sky. Then he reached into his money pouch and pulled out ten gold pieces. "Here."

Hobart took the ten gold, then went to his smallest lockbox — the one that had both a physical padlock *and* a Lock Spell on it that would let him open it, but nobody else. Normally, Hobart didn't deal with magick — the Brotherhood of Wizards charged outrageously high rates for their spells — but for Barlin cigars, he was willing.

As he undid the padlock, he noticed that two Cloaks were lingering nearby. Probably there to talk to him about the Kenspals.

He pulled one of his last batch of Barlin cigars from the thermidor, re-locked the box, and then handed the cigar over to the elf, who grabbed it and immediately ran the length of the cheroot under his nose. And then he smiled again, but this was a much more pleasant smile — more like the cat *after* he ate the mouse…

"*Felshariel sevtha.*"

"Okay." Hobart knew, maybe, four words in Ra-Telvish, the elves' tongue — five, if you counted *bahrlan* — and neither of those were it.

The elf then bowed. "Thank you, Hobart. I look forward to enjoying this."

As he moved off, the two Cloaks then moved toward him. To his relief, it wasnn't Tresyllione and ban Wyvald — they were always a pain in his posterior. To his annoyance, it wasn't Manfred and Kellan, either — those two were always good for a laugh. No, it was the former Shranlaseth and her new partner, the recently promoted Ocly.

"Lieutenants, what can I do for ya? Oh, and hey, Dannee, congrats on the promotion!"

Ocly grinned under her considerable facial hair. "Thank you, Hobart, that's very kind!" And she sounded like she meant it. Hobart had always liked Ocly.

Which was good, as Ocly's pleasant demeanor made being around the Shranlaseth much easier. He'd been hearing things about Aleta lothLathna since she first joined up a few years ago, most of which were probably not true, but every one of which made Hobart fear for the ability of his neck bones to stay intact in her presence.

"So what did you *really* just sell that elf? A Cormese cigar? One from Treemark, perhaps?"

"Do I look like an idiot?"

Giving him a smile that challenged her fellow elf's for its resemblance to predator feeding on prey, lothLathna replied, "Do you really want me to answer that, Hobart?"

"Look, I'll admit, I sold *plenty* a cigars to shitbrains for ten gold by tellin' 'em they's Barlin cigars, but not that guy. That's a customer who *knows* the merchandise, and he woulda known the second he put the stogie under his nose whether or not it was legit Barlin."

Ocly looked at lothLathna. "Did he just admit to committing a crime?"

"He did," lothLathna said with a smirk, "because he's afraid that if he ever lies to me, I'll break his neck. Which is not *quite* true."

Hobart's eyes widened. Was the Shranlaseth actually softening on him?

Then she continued: "I would break his clavicle. He can't learn from his mistake if I kill him, but it'd take *months* for that to heal, and it would be *extremely* painful."

Nope, not softening at all.

"Wow," Ocly said. "Hobart's lied to me dozens of times. I mean, I expected it—when I had my first case here on the Way after I made lieutenant, Captain Dru warned me about Hobart."

That brought Hobart up short. "Wait, when you two were down 'ere for that donnybrook with those elves and dwarves a few months back—Dru warned you about *me*?"

"He did. Said you saw everything that went on here, but not to believe a word you say."

LothLathna said, "Oh, the first day after I transferred to Dragon, Sergeant Grint warned me about you, too."

Hobart was torn between being honored that the higher-ups at the Castle Guard knew enough of him to speak so directly about him or being disgusted that the higher-ups at the Castle Guard knew him well enough to speak so plainly about him.

"But," lothLathna went on, "you *do* see everything that goes on here, as the captain told Dannee here, and we need to know about something that we've been told. Specifically, that there's a security force that's collecting money down here, apparently?"

Hobart did not reply immediately, as he needed to consider his response carefully.

Were it any of the other detectives—or Ocly by herself—that would've been one thing, but he really didn't want his clavicle broken, so he needed to be honest.

However, he also now had a new piece of information. Everyone 'round the Way just assumed that Ankh was being done with the full knowledge and cooperation of the Swords and Cloaks. Hobart could *definitely* make use of this new information that that wasn't the case at all.

"Yeah, it started up a buncha months back, after all the *bahrlans* came pourin' into town. Ankh Security, it's called—and it was one'a you lot that started it."

"A guard runs it?" Ocly asked, surprised.

"Retired guard, but yeah. Rob Wirrn."

Frowning, Ocly said, "He's one of the ones who got early retirement, right?"

"Early retirement?" Hobart laughed. "Didn't think the noble knobs let you do that kinda thing."

"Just one noble knob," lothLathna said. "During the mercifully brief reign of Lord Blayk, he gave several veterans the opportunity to retire early with full pensions. He was trying to make the Castle Guard younger, probably in order to turn them into an army to overthrow the king and queen."

Hobart nodded. "Right, I heard he was boiled in oil for tryin' a kill the monarchs."

"Rob was one of the ones who took that early retirement. So was Lieutenant Iaian."

"Was wonderin' why I ain't seen Iaian's ugly face lately." Hobart chuckled. "Anyhow, I guess Wirrn didn't like retirement that much, 'cause he started up those Ankh shitbrains."

"I'm guessing you don't like them?"

"Look, I pay my taxes." Strictly speaking, that wasn't true, but Hobart did pay bribes to particular representatives in the castle, so it amounted to the same thing. "That's supposed to pay for you Swords and Cloaks t'keep us safe. I mean, sure, shit got worse lately once we got all those bahrlans comin' in, but so what? Happened a dozen years ago when the war ended, too. Crime went up for a year, then it went back to normal again. So why I gotta pay extra to some retired guard t'do the same thing we're already payin' for? An' it's worse for the *bahrlans*."

For most of Hobart's rant, lothLathna barely seemed to be paying attention, which Hobart found rude but in character. But his last comment got her attention. "How is it worse for the refugees?"

"Wirrn's chargin' 'em more than 'e is reg'lar Cliff's End folk."

"Weren't you born in Iaron?" lothLathna asked.

"That ain't the point," Hobart said nervously. In fact, he was born in Treemark, but he was raised in Iaron. His father had thrown him out for getting the both of them into a bad investment scheme when Hobart was sixteen, and he'd fled to Cliff's End lest he incur the wrath of the other investors, who were prepared to do far worse than simply deny Hobart a place to live...

"Thank you, Hobart," Ocly said. "This was helpful."

"We may be back with more questions," lothLathna said, "and because you were so helpful we won't tell Mr. lothReshra that you have two dozen Barlin cigars, not five."

Hobart felt the blood drain from his face; he'd never even gotten the elf's name, yet she…. "How did you—"

But lothLathna just smiled as she and her partner walked away. Ocly, at least, favored him with a wave and a "Bye" as they departed.

Shaking his head, Hobart went and checked to make sure the small lockbox with the thermidor was secure.

Damn Cloaks…

SIX

As Torin and his partner entered the Old Ball and Chain following their shift, he found himself remembering the day seven years ago when the owner, Urgoss, then a guard from Dragon Precinct, was nearly killed.

A guild hall had collapsed in the midst of a Tavern Guild meeting, and the Castle Guard had been tasked with rescue operations. It was all hands on deck, as it were, and Torin, Danthres, Linder, Iaian, Karistan, and Nael were all tasked with helping pull people from the wreckage, alongside guards from all the precincts. Urgoss, a dwarf, had been pulling a Tavern Guild woman from underneath a pile of bricks that had fallen on her and shattered her leg. At that point, a support beam gave way, and the ceiling collapsed. Urgoss had barely managed to avoid it, but it had been a near thing.

The week before, Urgoss had reached his twenty-fifth year in the Guard, but had declined the pension to continue in the job. After nearly having a ceiling fall on him, he reversed that position and filed his retirement paperwork. Iaian and Geff Linder had been assigned to investigate what happened at the guild hall—it had been sabotage by the Blacksmith's Guild—and, at the two lieutenants' urging, Urgoss had been the one to arrest the guild leader who had ordered the job done.

That was Urgoss's last task as a member of the Castle Guard. He used his savings and his pension to purchase a tavern, which he renamed the Old Ball and Chain, after his grandfather, who was a general in the dwarven army. During his time as a soldier, Grandfather had carried a mace that he always referred to as the Old Ball and Chain. Urgoss's father had always said he was going to open a tavern with that name in honor of his Dad, but he drank himself to death instead.

Torin and Danthres worked their way to the back corner where the detectives usually sat in the evenings. It was Iaian and Linder who had first claimed that table after the tavern opened seven years ago, and it had been their table ever since. (Some guards from Goblin Precinct had tried to take it over it once, but Urgoss himself had made it clear to them that they weren't to sit there—mostly by delaying and watering down their drinks and messing up their orders until they finally changed tables.)

As he moved with Danthres through the long tables, Torin thought back to how completely the detective squad had changed since Urgoss opened this place. Linder and Nael had both been killed, with Nael's partner Karistan maimed, losing her arm, in the same assault that killed her partner. Iaian had retired, as had their boss Captain Osric, during Lord Blayk's brief regime. Others had come and gone. Hawk, killed during a bank robbery. Dru, promoted to captain. Amilar Grovis, who left to join the family business of running the Cliff's End Bank. Horran, brutally injured during the Gorvangin Rampages.

And now only Danthres and Torin were still with the squad.

Danthres said, "I'll get the drinks—ale?" Urgoss never hired waitstaff—he felt that you should come to the bar to get your drink, and if you were too drunk to manage that, then you should go home.

"Please," Torin said, and he proceeded to the table.

While Captain Dru hadn't joined them—he only did occasionally—the rest of the squad was all present. Manfred and Kellan were both nursing ales, while Dannee was throwing back a flagon of the fruity concoction she loved that Torin could smell from here. Aleta had a shot of that purple elven drink she favored.

Manfred grinned at Torin's approach. "And now the gang's all here!"

"Well," Kellan said, "once Danthres comes with the drinks. She couldn't've come by and asked what we wanted?"

"You all have drinks," Torin said as he sat next to Aleta. Doing so meant that he'd be a buffer between Aleta and Danthres, which was sometimes a dangerous place to be, but generally things went more smoothly if the elf who used to murder halfbreeds as a matter of course wasn't right next to the halfbreed.

Danthres came back with two flagons and sat next to Torin, placing the flagons down on the wooden table with a satisfying thunk.

"Good," Dannee said, "now we can ask them, too."

"Ask us what?" Torin queried while Danthres just started chugging her beer.

Aleta asked the question. "How well do you know Rob Wirrn?"

"I encountered him a few times," Torin said. "Good guard, always seemed to know everyone."

After finishing her gulp of ale and letting out a very loud belch, Danthres said, "I served with him in Goblin when I was a rookie. Torin's right, he always knew everyone on the street he walked past."

"He's one of the ones Blayk talked into retiring, as I recall," Torin said after sipping his own ale.

Aleta said, "Well, apparently he's started a security force to keep order down Jorbin's Way. It's called Ankh Security."

Torin frowned. "Isn't that what we're supposed to be for?"

Dannee pointed at Torin. "That's what I said!"

"Are you sure about this?" Danthres asked.

"Our victim mentioned it," Aleta said, "and Hobart confirmed it."

Danthres winced. "Hobart's not exactly a reliable source."

"He is for me." Aleta smiled proudly. "He's convinced that if he ever lies to me, I'll break his clavicle."

"And he hasn't lied to you once?" Torin asked.

"Not that I've discovered," Aleta said.

"Well, it works out either way." Danthres grinned. "Either you get good information, or Hobart suffers great pain. Win-win."

Manfred gulped down his drink, then said, "We haven't heard anything about this, either."

"Have you talked to Wirrn?" Torin asked.

Dannee shook her head. "We haven't had a chance. We got the confirmation about this Ankh Security while Boneen was doing the peel-back of our crime scene. Then we had to go try to find the people who trashed the stall, but we didn't have much to go on."

"Why, was the peel-back interfered with?" Torin asked.

"No, they wore masks."

Torin's face fell. "Please tell me they weren't hobgoblin masks."

"How'd you know that?" Dannee asked, sounding incredulous.

Exchanging an annoyed glance with Danthres, Torin answered the question. "The quartet who committed our murder last night were all wearing hobgoblin masks."

Dannee and Aleta exchanged a similar glance, though theirs was more shock. "We also had four people," Dannee said, "and the masks were all different colors."

"Red, yellow, orange, and green," Aleta said.

"Same as ours." Danthres pounded a fist on the table. "Dammit. I take it your victim was from Barlin?"

Aleta nodded.

"We should go to Dru tomorrow," Torin said, "and figure out how to proceed. Since the perpetrators are the same in our two cases, we may need to join forces."

"Joy," Danthres muttered. To Torin's relief, that was all she said.

Dannee said, "The captain may want us to look more into Ankh Security, though."

"Somebody should," Kellan muttered.

Chuckling, Danthres said, "I wish you'd told us this sooner, then we could've made you two talk to the Fansarris."

Manfred visibly shuddered. "Not the Fansarris…"

"You know them?" Torin asked.

"About a year and a half ago — when Gan Brightblade and his elven wizard friend were killed? I was working Unicorn then, and I got called to the Fansarris' house because a dimensional portal opened up in their back yard. A hobgoblin came out and nearly killed me."

Torin recalled the incident. "Wasn't it the Fansarris' son who conjured the portal?"

Manfred nodded.

"Interesting, as Elmira Fansarri said she had no children."

"If I remember right," Manfred said, "the brotherhood censured him, then they later decided to pull the censure as long as the kid studied to become a wizard all proper-like. He went off to their crazy-ass wizard academy on Jirrt Isle. The Fansarris *hate* magick, so it doesn't surprise me that they disowned him if he went off to apprentice to some wizard."

"Something the Fansarris and I have in common then," Danthres said with a chuckle. Her disdain for magick was legendary. "I wouldn't have believed it."

"Oi, ban Wyvald, Tresyllione!" came a voice from behind them.

Turning, Torin saw Hariella, who was one of the veterans who had transferred from Dragon to Phoenix when the latter was opened. She always insisted on working the night shift, from her time as a rookie in Unicorn. "Sun hurts my eyes," she always said.

Kellan laughed at her approach. "Shouldn't you be working, Hariella?"

"I *am* workin', Arn. Came 'ere for these two. Got us a *bahrlan* who got hisself beat up by the boulder by four shitbrains in hobgoblin masks—an' we know that 'cause this one lived and described 'em."

Torin's objection that they already had a case died on his lips. He looked at Danthres. "Same method of attack, same attackers, same type of victim, same location."

"But the victim lived. And the castle finally approved us taking overtime." Danthres gulped down the rest of her ale, let out a particularly loud belch even by her high standards, and then got up from the table. "Let's go."

SEVEN

THE BAD NEWS, AS FAR AS DANTHRES WAS CONCERNED, WAS THAT THE VICTIM was unable to provide a description that was any better than what they'd already got from Boneen's peel-back of Tuchera's assault, down to the exact colors of the four hobgoblin masks and the fact that one of them was noticeably shorter than the others (so likely a dwarf, gnome, or halfling). When shown the crystal with the image of the four of them that Boneen had provided, the victim, whose name was Amharo, confirmed that they were the four who assaulted her.

The good news was that at least this meant it was only one band of roving masked shitbrains beating up on refugees. That meant, Danthres hoped, that when they arrested these four for the murder of Tuchera, the assault on Amharo, and the vandalism to that stall down Jorbin's Way, this would be over.

She didn't entirely *believe* that, but she did hope it…

Amharo was leaning against the boulder. A healer had come by while she was waiting for Hariella to fetch Torin and Danthres from the Chain, so she was no longer covered in cuts and scrapes, though there were still a few small bruises. In truth, though, only the ripped state of her clothing remained as evidence that she was attacked.

"You know what's ridiculous, Lieutenant?" Amharo asked Danthres.

"Besides all of it?" Danthres asked wryly.

Amharo nodded in assent to her point, and then said, "I was actually born here in Cliff's End. I moved to Barlin twenty years ago when I met my husband. He—" Her voice caught. "He died in the fire. I came to Cliff's End with our kids, but the only place I could afford to live was here in New Barlin." She shook her head. "It's funny, I thought I'd be safe from all the attacks at the boulder, being from Cliff's

End originally, but I guess all the—" She sighed. "—the *bahrlans* are fair game."

Danthres shot a look at Torin. "What do you mean, 'all the attacks'?"

"It seems like every other night, I've been hearing about somebody getting jumped by the boulder."

"Really? We'll have to look into that." Danthres looked over at Hariella. "Can you escort her home?"

Nodding, Hariella said, "Sure. C'mon, ma'am."

Amharo gently pushed herself off the boulder. Danthres moved closer to catch her in case she stumbled, but she stayed upright on her own power. "Thank you, Lieutenants. I hope you find those fiends."

"We'll do our best," Danthres said.

Amharo nodded, and then walked slowly with Hariella the rest of the way down Boulder Pass to Albin Way.

Torin approached Danthres and said, "Since it's night anyhow, let's head over to the precinct house. Perhaps Sergeant Kaplan will be of more use than Slaney was."

Jerking a thumb behind her in the general direction of the Chain, Danthres said, "The flagon of ale I just finished is of more use than Slaney ever will be. But yes, it's worth a shot."

The four of them all walked into New Barlin. Danthres and Torin went right on Albin Way, while Hariella and Amharo went left.

"It's unusually quiet," Torin said.

Danthres, too, had noticed how few people were on the streets, and that small number was being quiet and quick. It was a marked contrast to the more crowded thoroughfares of Dragon Precinct that they had navigated to get here, which were full of slow-moving, loud people.

"They're scared," Danthres said. "And I don't blame them. This can't continue."

"I'm worried that Dru won't be able to talk Lord Doval out of a curfew at this rate."

"What would be the point? Look around." Danthres indicated the near-empty road with one arm. "The equivalent of a curfew is already in place: everyone's hiding in their homes, afraid to go out. And it's not doing a damn bit of good."

When they arrived at Phoenix Precinct, the contrast with their last trip was stark. Sergeant Ander Kaplan was sitting calmly at the sergeant's desk, and instead of chaotic running around, the guards of the precinct who were present were sitting quietly at their desks.

"Tresyllione, ban Wyvald," he said with a nod. "Good t'see ya. What brings you to Albinton?"

Danthres exchanged an amused glance with Torin. "I think you're the first person I've heard call this neighborhood by its proper name in months."

"New directive from the castle." Kaplan shrugged. "Don't call 'em *bahrlans*, and don't call it 'New Barlin.' Just doin' what I'm told. Mind you, I'm fine with the first one. Shouldn't be slurrin' the folks we're supposed to be protectin'."

"Good for you," Danthres said.

"As for what brings us to New Barlin—or, rather," Torin added with a grin, "Albinton, we were wondering if you could tell us about the roving band of mask-wearing brigands who've been assaulting refugees."

"According to our victim, it's been a regular occurrence near the boulder at night."

Kaplan frowned. "Really? I haven't noticed any reports of that. Maybe one or two incidents—and that murder last night—but I ain't heard nothin' beyond that."

"Our victim," Torin said, "says she has heard of many such incidents."

"It may be, ban Wyvald," Kaplan said with a sigh. "Folks 'round here ain't exactly trustin' of the Castle Guard. Ain't nothin' like it in Barlin, remember. It's as like as not that folks got attacked and didn't report it. Might not've even *known* to report it. I mean, we keep tellin' people that we're here to stop crimes like this, but they don't listen. An' why should they? They don't know who we are or nothin'."

A thought occurred to Danthres. "Is there a guard who's assigned to that beat?"

Nodding, Kaplan said, "Most nights it's Ungrilig, but it's his night off."

"Interesting," Torin said.

"What's interesting?" Danthres asked.

"Ungrilig is another one who was offered early retirement, like Rob Wirrn was. But he didn't take it."

Kaplan nodded. "Yeah, I asked him about that when he transferred over. Said he was worried he'd be bored."

Snorting, Danthres said, "He should be so lucky."

"We'll track him down tomorrow." Torin then snapped his fingers. "Oh, and also if you could have some guards check out the residence of one Gedling on Central Way — lives next door to our murder victim."

"What's he got to do with this? He a witness?"

"After a fashion," Torin said dryly. "He was sick and Tuchera was filling in for him. Had Gedling not gotten sick, *he* would've been the one walking home on Boulder Pass last night, and he might be dead right now. Given that this is the only one of these attacks that has resulted in a death—"

"So far," Danthres muttered bitterly.

Giving his partner a nod, Torin repeated, "So far, yes — it's possible that Tuchera wasn't even the target, that Gedling was."

Kaplan scoffed. "I doubt that. Seems t'me that Tuchera was targeted 'cause'a where he used to live, and they'd've gone after anyone."

"Perhaps, but Tuchera is the only one who was killed — thus far," he added with another nod to Danthres, "and the discrepant part of a set is always the one most worth investigating."

Danthres chuckled. "More of that great Myverin education you keep boasting about."

"So it's true," Kaplan said, rubbing his bearded chin. "You really are from Myverin, ban Wyvald?"

Laughing, Torin said, "Eleven years in Cliff's End, and I still get asked that."

"Well, it's just that I also heard that you served with Captain Osric during the war, and I just wasn't sure which was true."

"Both," Torin said. "Yes, I grew up in Myverin, including attending the Collegium, as Danthres indicated. But I grew weary of a philosopher's life, and longed for something more adventurous. I got significantly more adventure than I bargained for when I joined the human army during the war against the Elf Queen, serving under General Osric, as he was then. After the war, I came to Cliff's End, was reunited with Osric, and here I am."

Kaplan shook his head and chuckled. "All these years, I been wonderin' which story was true, and they both are. That's just—" He chuckled again. "Weird world we live in, innit?"

"Indeed."

"Anyhow, Ungrilig lives in that boarding house on Stone Path and Alfar's Way. Should be able to find him there tomorrow."

The timechimes rang midnight as Kaplan said those words.

"We've pushed the limit of even approved overtime at this point," Torin said.

"Assuming it really is approved," Danthres said bitterly. "Assuming Sir Rommett or some other shitbrain on the other side of the castle will decide to *un*-approve it, and we'll have to take a morning off next week or some other nonsense."

Torin smiled. "Either way, we should call it a night. Thank you for your help, Sergeant."

Kaplan bowed slightly. "My pleasure."

"You're certainly doing a better job than your counterpart on the day shift." Even as Danthres said those words, she saw Torin wince. He probably thought it was bad form to insult Kaplan's colleague. And it was, truly, but Danthres also didn't really care about form that much, good or bad, and Torin damn well knew that...

"I would never speak ill of a fellow sergeant in the Castle Guard," Kaplan said very loudly and formally. Then he grinned. "But I would also never contradict a lieutenant in the Guard, neither."

"Good night, Sergeant," Torin said, and the pair of them exited Phoenix Precinct.

Once they were back on Albin Way, circling back to Boulder Pass, Danthres said, "You want to come back to my place? It's closer and we can go straight to bed."

Torin opened his mouth, then closed it again.

"You want to wait for Jak, don't you?" she asked.

"He might come by tonight, and I don't want him to—"

"Go through what you've gone through *every night* lately? Look, he hasn't been showing up at all at your apartment, so the chances of his doing so tonight are ridiculously low."

Wryly, Torin said, "That's not exactly how probabilities work, but—"

Danthres, however, wasn't about to let him go off on a pedantic aside. "And even if, by some miracle, he breaks with recent tradition and does show, then he'll find the same empty bed that you've found all week. Which is, frankly, no less than he deserves."

Torin let out a long sigh that almost modulated into a moan. "I do not wish to be so—so mean."

"It's only mean if he shows up. Probabilities be damned, Torin—do you really think he'll show tonight?"

The silence that came from her partner spoke volumes to Danthres.

After he didn't reply for the better part of a minute, Danthres said, "Exactly. So come home with me. You'll probably sleep better."

"I doubt that," Torin muttered. Then more loudly: "But I shall. If for no other reason than I'm exhausted, and it'd be an extra twenty-minute walk to my place."

"Good." Danthres and Torin had been occasional lovers since two years into their partnership, following a particularly exhausting shift when midsummer coincided with Wiate's Moon Festival. In the nine years since, they'd been occasional bedmates, though sometimes they simply slept together.

Given Torin's last comment, as well as Danthres's own fatigue, she suspected that would be the case tonight.

Tomorrow, they would talk to Ungrilig, and with any luck get some insight into what had been happening at Boulder Pass.

EIGHT

"I GOTTA TELL YOU, MANFRED, I AM JUST LOVING MY LIFE."

As they walked down Meerka Way through the tree-lined thoroughfares and mansions of Unicorn Precinct, heading toward a call in Dragon Precinct, Manfred looked at his partner Arn Kellan quizzically. "Excuse me?"

"Life. It's good. Don't you think it's good?"

"You had sex last night, didn't you?"

That brought Kellan up short. "I didn't, actually. No, Emrys said he wants to slow things down. No, I'm just—" He shook his head. "Look, I grew up dirt-poor in Goblin. Me, two brothers, four sisters, our parents, and three grandparents in a shitty shack on Kite Path. Now look at me. I got a nice place in Dragon, and I'm a damn *lieutenant* in the Castle Guard."

"I'm guessin' Mom, Dad, and the three grandparents are all proud?"

"Grandparents an' Dad are all dead, and Mom could give a shit."

Manfred winced. "Sorry, partner."

"S'okay. There's a good reason why I don't talk about my family much. Mom's still in the same shitty shack all by herself. Still cleanin' up the Stone Kobold every mornin'. They pay enough t'keep her payin' rent and buyin' cheap booze."

They crossed Oak Way into Dragon Precinct. Manfred hesitated before posing his next question. "You mind if I ask what happened to your six siblings?"

"Nah, I don't mind. It ain't that I'm embarrassed, I just don't like talkin' about 'em, y'know?"

"I get it. It's just we've been partners for a year, we've been friends since we both signed up four years ago, and you know all about *my* stupid family."

Kellan grinned. "Even met a few of 'em."

Manfred shuddered, remembering the midsummer feast that his aunt and uncle tried to put together, that Manfred ill-advisedly invited Kellan along to. It was an open question what was worst, the burnt roast, the way his uncle Calvin was hitting on all the women at the dinner, his father's terrible jokes, the braying laugh his mother always used when he told those terrible jokes, or that Aunt Freia kept calling Kellan "Arnie-kins" no matter how many times he asked her not to.

Counting off siblings on his fingers, Kellan said, "Let's see, the oldest was Ava, an' she hopped a caravan to Iaron when she turned sixteen because they said they had a big job for people who could sew, and she could sew. Ain't heard nothin' from her since. Dunno if she's alive, dead, or sewin' up a storm in Iaron, or what. Alvo's doin' time on the barge for robbery."

Wincing, Manfred asked, "You didn't arrest him, did you?"

Kellan shook his head. "I was only six when he got arrested."

"He's *still* on the barge?" Manfred was incredulous. The prison barge, which was now part of the Castle Guard and dubbed Manticore Precinct, was where the prisoners who weren't condemned to death were incarcerated. "Twenty-plus years is a lot for a robbery."

"He robbed a nobleman who was visitin' from Velessa on behalf'a the king and queen. He's still got ten years t'go." Kellan shook his head. "Alvo never was too bright. Anyhow, Ariana an' Ana both got married and are raisin' kids in their own hovels on Kite Path. They ain't talkin' t'me or Mom. That just leaves the twins — they're the youngest. Abner and Alia."

"Noticin' a naming pattern there, *Arn*."

Holding up both hands, Kellan said, "Don't look at me, that was Mom and Dad's stupid thing. Anyhow, Abner was workin' as a stable boy in Unicorn till he got his head kicked in by a horse he was too stupid t'handle right, an' Alia signed on as a cook on the *Letashia*. She went down in a hurricane a buncha years back."

They turned onto Haven's Path, heading toward the Corner Eatery. Manfred was sorry he'd asked the question. Two of Kellan's siblings were dead, one was on the barge, and the other three were incommunicado. And his mother, apparently, was a drunk. *No wonder he never talks about family.*

As if reading his mind, Kellan said, "Don't be sorry you asked. The family ain't me, I'm me. An' like I said, I'm happy. I got a great job,

Emrys an' I are doin' great, even if he does wanna back off a bit, an' I got a great partner."

Manfred grinned. "Well, I'm happy too. I got a great job—no boyfriend or girlfriend or nothin', but that's fine, I'm good like I am. Yeah, my family's nuts, but I love 'em. An' you're right—*you* got a great partner."

Playfully punching Manfred on the arm, Kellan said, "Shitbrain."

"I'm just glad neither of us won the bet."

"Yeah. Never did get to tell Osric about that." When they were both guards, Dru's predecessor Osric had told both Manfred and Kellan that they were being groomed for promotion to lieutenant as soon as there was an opening in the detective squad. The pair of them had a bet going as to who would get promoted first—but then there were three openings at once, so they both got promoted together, along with Aleta.

They arrived at the Corner Eatery, where a bunch of guards from Dragon were gathered. Manfred recognized two guards he'd served with in Unicorn back in the day.

"Hey Kamno, Lofriqa! When'd you guys move to Dragon?"

Lofriqa grinned a gap-toothed smile. "When Phoenix opened up, we got us moved over. Ain't no more dealin' with rich arses and their stupid-ass problems. Now it's poor arses and *their* stupid-ass problems, ain't that right, Kamno?"

"Yeah."

Manfred chuckled. These two hadn't changed a bit. "This is my partner, Arn Kellan."

"Oh yeah, you used t'work Goblin, right? We used t'work Goblin, too, but that was ages ago, ain't that right, Kamno?"

"Yeah."

"Didja work with Allard and Brenn?"

Kellan nodded. "Yeah, they—"

"Coupla crazy old arses, those two. Why, I remember one time when they was rookies and—"

Manfred held up a hand before Lofriqa went off on another one of her rants, periodically punctuated by monosyllabic utterances by Kamno. "What've we got here, Lofriqa?"

"Oh right, the crime. Sorry, got carried away seein' ya. I'm always gettin' carried away, ain't that right, Kamno?"

"Yeah."

Lofriqa walked over to the tables set outside the Corner Eatery. A young man was being tended to by a dwarven healer.

As they approached, the healer looked up and at Manfred and Kellan. "Are you two in charge?"

Manfred exchanged a quick look with Kellan and then said slowly, "Uh, we're the lieutenants in charge of this investigation, and we—"

"Good. That means when you're done, you're going back to the castle, right?"

"Eventually," Manfred said.

"Sometimes we get enough info t'go after the perpetrator," Kellan said.

"Either way, I'm staying with the two of you until you go back to the castle so I can present an invoice to Sir Rommett *in person*, and you two will accompany me."

"Uh, ma'am," Manfred started, "that's not our—"

The healer held up a hand. "I don't want to hear it. With this gentleman here, I'm now owed twenty-six silver by the castle for helping people at crime scenes. The Castle Guard used to pay me on time, but now I've got invoices going back *months*. This is the last time I heal someone at a crime scene until I get paid."

"Glad I made the cut." That was the victim, who was rubbing his face.

"You're lucky," the dwarf said. "I was already having lunch here. Otherwise, I wouldn't have bothered."

"Look," Manfred said, "can you go sit over there? We need to actually investigate this crime. I promise, we won't give you the slip, and you can come back to the castle with us."

"Fine." The dwarf turned and walked over to one of the other tables and sat down.

The proprietor of the Corner came over, then. A tall willowy elf, with an apron over his tunic and tights, he looked vexed. "Manfred, Kellan, good to see you. Can I reopen, please?"

Kellan rolled his eyes. "C'mon, Thrithshar, you know it don't work like that. We just got here, we don't even know what happened."

The victim said, "I'm the one who got beat up, and *I* don't know what happened!"

Putting up a hand to interrupt Thrithshar saying something else, Manfred said, "Let us talk to the man, and then we'll see what we can do, okay?"

Turning to the victim, Kellan asked, "What's your name, sir?"

"Jahn Tristan."

"And what happened?"

"I have no idea!" Tristan sighed. "Look, I was just sitting here, eating one of Thrithshar's pastries and drinking tea, and all of a sudden, some malefactor walks up to me and *hits* me. A lot!"

"Did you recognize him?" Manfred asked.

"Never seen him before."

Thrithshar said, "I have."

Manfred whirled to face the elf. "You know who attacked him?"

"Yes, he comes by here sometimes. I don't know where he lives, but his name is Worlin. He's human, short, stocky, curly brown hair, flat nose."

"I don't suppose you know where he lives?"

"He complained last week about the noise coming from the guild hall across the street. Said they'd been partying for three straight nights."

Manfred looked at Kellan and smiled. "All right, thanks. I think you can open back up."

Emphatically, Thrithshar said, "*Thank* you, Lieutenants."

Kellan looked at Tristan. "Mr. Tristan, if we arrest Worlin, are you willing to testify before the magistrate that he assaulted you?"

"Absoltuely, I'll testify. The name's Jahn Tristan as I said, and I live on Maple Path."

"That's in Unicorn Precinct," Manfred said.

"Yes, what of it?"

Looking at Kellan briefly, Manfred then said, "Well, sir, your clothes are nice enough, but not—not of the quality you usually get from folks that live in Unicorn."

Tristan rolled his eyes. "I guess that's why they call you detectives. I manage the Magick Shop on Maple Path, and one of the perks is an apartment over the shop." He snorted. "The wizard who owns the shop isn't interested in the minutiae of the management of the shop, he's only interested in the coin it produces. I asked if I could live in the apartment over the shop, and he allowed it. Saves me a ton on rent."

"I bet." Kellan chuckled.

"And it means I can afford these." He held up a pastry that Manfred didn't recognize. "Damn near impossible to get Frelain pastries ever since the fire. Had a regular customer from Barlin bring some by the shop, and I've been addicted to the things ever since. One of these days, I'm going to go to Barlin and have them there—I'm told they're much better in the city-state itself. I mean, I won't be going there any time soon, but some day, when things are better…"

Kellan must have seen the confused look on Manfred's face, because he came to his rescue. "Frelain's a Barlin style of pastry-makin'. Hard t'get the ingredients these days."

"I bet," Manfred said. "All right, we'll be in touch, Mr. Tristan."

Manfred then turned to head back toward Meerka Way, both Kellan and the healer following.

"You're leaving so soon?" the healer asked.

"We have what we need," Manfred said. "And we don't want to keep the place closed any longer than necessary."

"Aren't you supposed to wait for the magickal examiner?"

"You know 'bout that?" Kellan asked, sounding surprised.

"I've done a *lot* of your crime scenes."

"Well," Kellan said, "we got us a victim who remembers what happened, and we got us a witness who provided a real good description. So we can go an' find an' arrest the bad guy."

"How do you know that the elf's description was accurate? He could've been lying to get you to leave and reopen faster."

Now it was Manfred who rolled his eyes. *Elves and dwarves…* "The Corner's *real* popular with the guards. Thrithshar lies to us, we let everyone know, and then the guards stop coming here."

"He ain't gonna piss off his best customers," Kellan added.

They reached Meerka Way, and turned right, heading toward Celinda Path. "All the M.E. would do is provide an account of what happened and a description of the perpetrators, but we already *have* that. So now we don't have to deal with a cranky old wizard."

"An' any day we ain't gotta deal with Boneen's nonsense is a *good* day."

The healer nodded. "That makes sense. Wizards are a pain. So how do you know where to go now? The elf only said he lived across from a guild hall, and there are a dozen of those."

Kellan grinned. "Yeah, but only one of 'em had a three-night party last week."

Within a few minutes, they arrived at Celinda Path, on the corner of which was the hall shared by the Cooper's Guild and the Lumber Guild.

The current heads of both guilds shared a birthday, and they celebrated it last week with a huge party. Sergeant Jonas had told them to be on the lookout for problems relating to that, but they'd kept to themselves, the only issues being noise complaints.

Across from the hall were two homes. They knocked on one, and it was answered by an elderly gnome woman who lived there alone.

The second door was opened by a short, stocky human with brown curly hair.

"Are you Worlin?"

"What if I am?"

"I'm Lieutenant Manfred, this is my partner, Lieutenant Kellan. We have reason to believe that you assaulted someone at the Corner Eatery earlier today."

"Didja arrest that *bahrlan?*"

That was not the answer Manfred had been expecting. "Excuse me?"

"The *bahrlan* I beat up, you arrest his ass?"

"So you admit to beating him up?" Manfred had to admit to being pleased — it was always easier when the perpetrators admitted to their crimes.

"Yeah, I beat the *bahrlan* up, he slept with my wife! Adultery's a crime, ain't it?"

"It ain't, actually," Kellan said.

"Troll-shit! Ghandurha says adultery's a sin, dammit!"

Manfred sighed. "That's something you'll need to take up with a priest. But the lord and lady's laws don't consider adultery to be a crime, though it can be used in divorce proceedings."

"Fine, I'll go to a priest, then."

"It'll have to wait until after you serve your time on the barge, Mr. Worlin."

"Say what?"

A woman came into view. "Worlin, what's going on?"

"They didn't arrest that *bahrlan* you fucked, that's what's goin' on, Paytra."

"Ma'am," Kellan said, "you're gonna have t'come with us, too. We're all headin' up to the castle t'sort this out."

From behind them, the healer said, "And sort out my problem, too!"

Manfred ignored the healer. "Worlin, I'm arresting you in the lord and lady's name for your assault on Jahn Tristan."

"Worth beatin' up that *bahrlan* after what he did to Paytra, I'll tell ya that."

Paytra threw up her hands. "For Ghandurha's sake, Worlin, you are such an idiot! I didn't sleep with that *bahrlan*!"

Worlin turned to face his wife. "Say *what*?"

"I just said he did it to shut you the hell up. I didn't think anything would come of it, since he's a *bahrlan*."

"He isn't, actually," Manfred said. "He just likes pastries from there."

"Really?" Paytra's face fell.

Kellan regarded her with annoyance. "Paytra, I'm arresting you in the lord and lady's name for conspiracy to commit assault on Jahn Tristan."

"Let's go," Manfred said.

Worlin was staring daggers at his wife. "You stupid bitch."

Paytra was ignoring him and muttering, "Thought for *sure* he was a *bahrlan*."

"Wouldn't'a mattered if he was," Kellan said as he led her out of the house, Manfred doing the same with Worlin. "It's still assault, an' still against the law."

"Hmp," Paytra said. "I thought the lord and lady's law just applied to folks from Cliff's End, not *bahrlans*."

"They apply to everyone *in* Cliff's End, ma'am," Manfred said. "C'mon, let's go."

NINE

"I'M SORRY, I'M NOT PAYING IT."

Jhim Hallam stood with his hands on his hips as he faced the dwarf and the troll standing on the other side of his vegetable stand. Both the very big troll and the very short dwarf wore ankh symbols on their tunics, and the troll was holding a box with an ankh emblazoned on the lid. The dwarf was named Obanag; Hallam had never learned the troll's name.

"You want our protection," Obanag said, "you gotta pay."

"What protection?" Hallam threw up his hands. "The Kenspals' stall was wrecked! The whole reason why I drop coins into that box every week is 'cause you people keep saying you're gonna keep us safe. Well, I know for a fact that Jora put coins into that box, and look what happened!"

"That was—"

Holding up a hand at the dwarf's face, Hallam said, "I don't want to hear it, Obanag."

The troll grunted and grabbed Hallam's wrist with the hand that wasn't holding the box.

"Ow!" The troll's grip was firm and painful, and Hallam tried and failed to pull out of it.

Obanag put a small hand on the troll's large arm. "All right, Brenfelk, that's enough, don't hurt him."

The troll, whose name was, apparently, Brenfelk, grunted again, but did not let go.

Then Obanag let loose with some gibberish, and Brenfelk finally released his grip on Hallam's wrist.

Pulling the now-very-sore wrist in and rubbing it, Hallam asked, "What did you just say?"

"Brenfelk pretends like he can't understand Common whenever I ask him to do something he don't wanna do, so I have to ask him in Hargit."

"Uh huh."

"Now look, Hallam, the protection we offer is *real*. I know that poor Jora Kenspal was hit, but—"

"Don't give me 'real,' Obanag. When I lived in Barlin, you know what I did?"

"Sold vegetables, I presume."

"Actually, I sold fruit and vegetables, all from Tomvale, but fruit doesn't travel as well, so I just stick with veggies now that I'm in Cliff's End. I get a shipment every morning. Anyhow, that's not what I meant. What I meant was that, in Barlin, I paid my taxes. And do you know what that meant?"

"The noble knobs in Barlin's castle got most'a your money?"

"Well, that's what it wound up meaning, but what they *told* me it meant was that we'd be protected. In fact, we were specifically told that some of our tax money went to the Brotherhood of Wizards to cast various spells that would keep the city-state safe. When that tornado blew through five years ago and trashed Tomvale and Treemark and Upper Nimvale, Barlin didn't get touched. And then, after the tornado? They raised our taxes. Said they needed stronger spells because they almost failed against the tornado, y'see. But it's okay, they said. We'll protect you, they said. Barlin protects Barlin—that was something the Lord himself told us."

"You talked to the Lord?" Obanag asked incredulously.

"Gave a speech in Phalin Park, as a matter of fact, during midsummer. And he promised us that everything'd be fine, it'd just be a little more expensive. So we dug into our pouches and we paid more. But then the fire happened. People died, and homes were lost, and did they protect us? Did they help us out? Did Barlin protect Barlin? No!"

Obanag started, "Look, this is all well and good, but—"

But Hallam had no interest in what the dwarf had to say. "I'm done, is what I'm saying. I've been taken in too many times, and I'm not letting it happen again. So go away, you're scaring my customers."

That last wasn't entirely true—it had been a slow day, and Obanag and Brenfelk had been the only people to approach Hallam's stall in the last half-hour—but no one was likely to come by with that troll standing right at the center of the table, blocking all access.

For several seconds, Obanag just stared at Hallam, who stared right back. He fixed his gaze on the dwarf, since he expected to lose a staring contest with a troll.

Finally, Obanag looked away, which Hallam considered to be a big victory.

Brenfelk, however, slammed the collection box onto a tiny blank spot on the table, between the ears of corn and the bell peppers. The thud of the box startled Hallam, and he switched his gaze to the troll.

"Hey!"

"Pay now!" Brenfelk said in a gravelly voice. "Pay now or get beat!"

Obanag wrapped both of his small hands around Brenfelk's huge left arm. "No, Brenfelk, no! We're not doing that!"

"You expect people to trust you to protect them when you threaten them like this?" Hallam asked frantically.

Now Obanag was pulling on the troll's arm. "Come, Brenfelk. Let us move on."

Brenfelk shook himself free of the dwarf, which nearly knocked Obanag over, then snatched the collection box. The troll snarled at Hallam, pointed at him, then walked off with Obanag.

Only then did Hallam let out the breath he'd been holding.

The next stall over was an herb and soap merchant named Bekka, who said, "You're makin' a mistake, you are."

Hallam sighed. "I already had this argument with Obanag, I don't want to have it with you, too."

"Fine, but you mark my words, you do, that they'll be some mischief happens t'yer stall 'fore too long, there will."

The rest of the day went decently. Mornings were usually slow in any event, but around lunchtime he started getting more customers, and by midafternoon, it was a constant stream of people, a good combination of new customers and regulars. He made sure to have the Crevin family's squash, Felthria lothHathor's corn, and Imbrilig's varieties of lettuce. Plus, there was a tourist who was in Cliff's End for a month who wanted to get her hands on Iaron artichokes. Which weren't actually artichokes, nor were they grown in Iaron, but Sohvi, Hallam's supplier, would be able to get them if he asked.

By the time he closed at sunset, most of the vegetables were gone, and as usual, Arolda from the Dog and Duck came by to buy up whatever was left to use in the kitchen for late-night meals.

"This all you got left?" Arolda asked, just like she always did.

"No, I'm hiding some under the table." Hallam rolled his eyes. "*Yes*, that's all I got left. It was a good day."

"So I can get all this for a copper piece, right?"

Hallam ground his teeth. *Every damn night.* "The deal I made with Olaf is for a silver for everything, no matter how much."

"But there was twice as much yesterday, and you only charged a silver."

"So you got a bargain last night." Hallam sighed. "Look, it's a silver or go back to Olaf and tell him you didn't get any vegetables, and when Seavi asks for more veggies and he doesn't get any—"

"Fine, fine, fine," Arolda said quickly. Seavi was another Barlin refugee who had worked at the Ruffing Tavern in Barlin, which was destroyed by the fire. He came to Cliff's End and was immediately hired by Olaf for the Dog and Duck. Already a popular spot thanks to being the place where legendary heroes Gan Brightblade and Olthar lothSirhans were both killed, Seavi's hiring made the Dog and Duck the place to get food in Dragon Precinct.

Which meant Seavi needed lots of vegetables, and if he didn't get them, he wouldn't cook certain dishes. Which would make everyone unhappy.

Digging into her money pouch, Arolda pulled out a silver piece and flicked it through the air. "Here you go."

Hallam caught it unerringly and then helped her pack up the vegetables into her cart.

Once the vegetables were cleared out, Hallam cleaned the table and then went home to sleep. On occasion, he would go for a drink, but he wasn't in the mood after dealing with those Ankh thugs this morning.

So he went straight home to his small room in a boarding house on Blarque Path. At first, he'd lived in New Barlin like everyone else, but when he found out about a room opening up in Dragon Precinct instead of the awful new neighborhood, he grabbed it. It was actually more expensive for less room, but it was only a few blocks from Jorbin's Way, and by not living in New Barlin, he could at least pretend he wasn't a "filthy *bahrlan*." Besides, he only needed a place to sleep. Most nights, he was too tired to do anything else, and it wasn't as if he ever entertained or anything like that.

The next morning, he got up before sun-up as usual and went with his wheelbarrow to the clearing in the Forest of Nimvale where carriages and caravans and such came from the other land-locked city-states, notably Tomvale. Just like he did every day, he waited for Sohvi to show up with her cart full of vegetables.

When she arrived, the two of them started transferring the vegetables from her cart to his wheelbarrow.

"Hey, Sohvi, can you get me some Iaron artichokes? I got a customer who wants a dozen."

"Sure. I can have 'em in two days."

"Good." That was what Hallam had told the tourist, and he just had to hope that she'd really come back the day after tomorrow to buy them.

If she didn't, he'd hold them back from Seavi's leftovers. Those things had a months-long shelf-life, thanks to a rock-hard skin, and he'd find *someone* to buy them...

He paid Sohvi, then worked his way down Meerka Way through the mansions of Unicorn Precinct and the shops and apartment buildings and guild halls of Dragon Precinct before arriving at Jorbin's Way—

—to find a pile of ashes where his stand had been the night before.

He dropped the wheelbarrow's struts onto the ground and just stared at the ashes that were his table.

"Shit."

Bekka came by with her own wagon. "I told you, I did!"

Hallam shook his head. "Can you watch my wheelbarrow, please?"

"I guess so, I can. Why for?"

"I need to find a guard."

"Okay."

He remembered seeing a couple of guards wandering at the corner of Jorbin's and Meerka Way when he came down. While he didn't remember their exact names—Hallam could always remember his customers' names, but he was terrible with names of people who didn't give him money in exchange for goods—he was damn sure going to talk to them now. These Ankh Security people needed to be stopped...

TEN

UNGRILIG LIMPED SLOWLY INTO THE SQUADROOM IN THE EAST WING OF THE castle just as the time chimes rang sixteen.

Sergeant Jonas came in from the pantry, shuffling parchments in his hands, his green cloak flowing behind him. Upon noticing the dwarf's entrance, he said, "Ungrilig! Good to see you! It's been a few years."

Chuckling, Ungrilig said, "More than a few, truth be told. I still remember when you first signed on and you couldn't find your way back to the precinct house every time you went on a call."

"Why do you think they made me a sergeant?" Jonas said with a smirk. "I never go out on calls anymore, and at this point, I've pretty much got the route from my house to the castle down pat."

"Glad to hear it. Leading search parties got real old real fast."

"What brings you here?" Jonas asked as he brought the parchments over to the picture window that looked out over the Forest of Nimvale.

"Got a note from Sergeant Kaplan saying that two of the lieutenants wanted to talk to me about something."

Jonas then looked at the window and said, "The Ferrio case."

The glass suddenly twisted and reformed into a face, an action that scared the hell out of Ungrilig, and almost caused him to lose his footing. "What in Xinf's name is *that*?"

"You've never seen Ep?" Jonas asked.

"What's an Ep?"

The face in the window said, "I'm not *an* Ep, I'm *the* Ep. I'm the imp that keeps the records for the Castle Guard."

"Oh." Ungrilig was more than a little nonplussed. He'd only been to the castle a few times, and had never seen this — this *thing* in action before.

Jonas put one of the parchments into the imp's mouth, and then the face contorted again, fading away until it was a window again.

Just then, Captain Dru exited his office, followed by Lieutenants Tresyllsione and ban Wyvald. "Ungrilig, you old bastard, good to see you."

Putting a hand over his heart and hoping that it was slowing down now that that Xinf-forsaken imp wasn't there anymore, Ungrilig said, "Afternoon, Dru. Sorry, *Captain*. Still can't get used to that."

Dru leaned forward and said, "Me either, t'be honest. Thanks for comin' up."

"Not like I had a choice," Ungrilig said with a sigh. "Sergeant said to come, I come."

Behind Dru, Tresyllione said, "Actually, *we* said to come. We just want to ask you about your beat in Phoenix."

"Sergeant Kaplan said you were the authority on the area around where Boulder Pass and Albin Way intersect," ban Wyvald added.

Ungrilig shrugged. "All right, I suppose."

Dru asked Jonas, "Where's everyone else?"

"Manfred and Kellan got a call to an assault at the Corner Eatery, and we got a murder in Mermaid, so I had to send Aleta and Dannee there."

Then ban Wyvald indicated the guest chair next to one of the desks. "Why don't we sit here and chat, Ungrilig, if that's all right?"

Ungrilig allowed himself to breathe a sigh of relief. From the moment he'd seen the note from Kaplan he'd been worried that he was in some kind of trouble. But no, they just wanted to talk to him. If he was in trouble, they'd put him in one of the interrogation rooms.

He took the seat, and ban Wyvald sat perpendicular to him. Tresyllione sat on the edge of ban Wyvald's desk on the other side of him, which Ungrilig appreciated. Ungrilig didn't actually have anything against elves personally, but they had a smell that he just couldn't *stand*. It wasn't as bad with Tresyllione—he was grateful that lothLathna wasn't the one assigned to this case, as he'd probably be gagging being stuck with her indoors—but still, the further away she was, the better.

"So we understand," ban Wyvald said, "that you declined the early retirement that Lord Blayk offered."

"Yeah, I figured I'd be bored. Been a guard for twenty years. I *like* being a guard. Like to serve the people."

"That's very noble of you," ban Wyvald said, and to Ungrilig's surprise, he sounded sincere in that statement.

"There's a satisfaction when you're walking a beat, knowing that you're keeping people safe. I really like that. No offense, but that's why I like being on the streets instead of here in the castle. Feel like I'm doing more good. Mostly because we're there all the time, so we can usually stop the bad stuff before it happens. Not like you detectives—you don't show up until after that bad stuff has gone down."

"It's good that you get such a sense of fulfillment," ban Wyvald said, "and no offense taken. I can see how you would find that a better use of your skills."

Tresyllione regarded ban Wyvald. "Plus, of course, the regular paycheck helps with all those gambling debts."

Ungrilig swallowed, and suddenly it felt much hotter in the squadroom. "Excuse me?"

"Would you like to know how we spent our morning, Ungrilig?" Tresyllione asked with a sweet smile that scared the shit out of Ungrilig.

"H-how?"

"Talking to residents of Phoenix Precinct, once your landlady told us you were still asleep and had asked for a fifteen wake-up."

"I—I don't get many days off," Ungrilig said slowly. "Gives me a chance to—to catch up on my sleep." He somehow managed not to ask how the *hell* they knew about his gambling problems. He hadn't told *anyone.*

"Imagine our surprise," ban Wyvald said, "when we were told that there have been multiple assaults near the boulder. We were especially surprised because those assaults hadn't been reported, at least according to Sergeants Slaney and Kaplan, who don't know anything about any assaults in that location besides the murder of Tuchera."

Tresyllione added, "The residents we spoke to were all *very* shocked that we knew nothing about it, too. 'We reported it,' they said. 'Talked to that dwarf guard,' they said. 'Ungrilig said he'd take care of it,' they said."

Still maintaining his friendly, conversational tone—unlike the snideness of his partner—ban Wyvald said, "This, of course, led us to wonder what possible reason a guard of your standing would have to cover up so many assaults."

Ungrilig shifted in his seat. He had no idea how much they knew, but anything he would say would just make things worse.

So he just sat quietly and let them talk.

"We talked to a few of your fellow guards in Phoenix Precinct," Tresyllione said, "plus some who worked with you in Dragon and Goblin, but they had nothing but the kindest things to say about you."

Unable to help himself, Ungrilig smiled, beaming with pride, knowing that his fellow guards spoke well of him.

"But then Sergeant Markon said something interesting to us," Tresyllione said very casually. "He told us to talk to Hanna Serviling."

Shit. Ungrilig tried to keep a straight face, but he should have known that Hanna wouldn't keep her damn mouth shut.

"She had a lot to say." Tresyllione stood up and walked over to sit on the corner of the desk that was on the other side of Ungrilig. Now he was surrounded, and worse, he had to put up with Tresyllione's odor.

"From what she told us," ban Wyvald said, "you've always had a particular affinity for those roving illegal hobgoblin races."

"More precisely," Tresyllione said, "that you had an affinity for betting very very poorly on them."

"I believe she mentioned dice as well," ban Wyvald added, as if he'd just remembered that, which Ungrilig doubted.

"Oh, she mentioned dice quite a bit." Tresyllione smiled unpleasantly, though he doubted that she ever smiled pleasantly. "After all, you still owe her, what, ten gold?"

"Fifteen, actually, with the interest."

Unable to help himself, Ungrilig muttered, "Bitch said she wouldn't charge interest!"

"Ah, so you do admit to borrowing money from her?" Tresyllione said triumphantly.

Ungrilig shut his eyes and exhaled slowly. After promising himself he wouldn't say anything and just let the lietuenants talk, so he wouldn't incriminate himself, and then he went and shot his mouth off, just because Hanna was so damned annoying.

No, that's not fair. Hanna helped me out and I never paid her back. That ain't her fault, it's mine.

"Look, I stopped gambling. I did!" He added that last when Tresyllione gave him a dubious expression. "I haven't picked up a pair of dice in a year, and there haven't even been any hobgoblin races since you guys locked Vanden up. But I still owe a ton of gold to a *lot* of people." He sighed. "Including Hanna. So when I got the offer to look the other way so they could beat up some *bahrlans*, I said yes, as long as they kept to my beat. I figured no one would even notice."

"Until they killed one," ban Wyvald said.

"That's the thing—that night? They paid extra."

Tresyllione frowned. "What do you mean?"

"They paid me five silvers every time they wanted me to let them do their business in peace, but the other night, they paid me a gold, said they were going after a *bahrlan* named Gedling."

At that, Tresyllione and ban Wyvald exchanged a surprised glance. It only happened for a second, but Ungrilig knew that kind of almost telepathic contact between partners. He'd had it with some of the guards he'd worked with over the last two decades.

Including Hanna, he thought with a sigh.

Tresyllione jumped off the desk and stood over Ungrilig. "Here's what's going to happen. You're going to tell us who paid you. You're going to tell us what other bribes you might have taken over the years. Then you're going to put in your retirement papers."

"I—" Ungrilig started to object, but he realized that nowhere in that list of events Tresyllione had listed did she mention his being arrested and put in the hole. That was a level of consideration not everyone got.

However, he needed to get *something* out of this. "Is this the same offer Lord Blayk gave me? Twenty-five-year pension? I'm only asking because there's no way I can pay off the rest of my debts—including to Hanna—unless I have *some* kind of income."

"You can always find another job," Tresyllione said.

"As what?" Ungrilig took a breath, realizing that snapping at the lieutenants was not a great career move right present. "I'm sorry, but—I can barely walk. Took me ninety minutes to get here from my home, and it would've been two hours if I came from the precinct house. Only reason I can still be a guard is because everyone knows me and cuts me some slack. But I need the money to pay everyone I owe off. That's why I took the payments—it helped me get rid of one of the creditors, and besides, I figured it was just more beating up *bahrlans*. It's been going on all over the place anyhow, whether I took the money to look the other way or not." He sighed. "Didn't expect anybody to get killed, though." He then looked ban Wyvald right in the eye. "But I can't do anything else, Lieutenant. I can barely do this. I need income."

After a moment, ban Wyvald said, "That's not a decision either of us can make. We'll have to take it up with the captain, who will have to bring it to the other wing of the castle."

"Oh, come on, Lieutenants, those wealthy bastards won't even notice."

Tresyllione snorted. "They absolutely will notice. Trust me, those wealthy bastards love to count their gold coins and recount them to make sure they're all there. And understand something." She loomed even more menacingly over him now, and Ungrilig swallowed twice. "You've always been a good, solid guard. I remember back when I was a rookie in Goblin, and all the shitbrains like Nulti and Slaney were riding my ass, you were always good to me, and actually helped me with some cases. That's why you're not in an interrogation room right now, and it's why we're giving you a shot at getting out of this without a trip to the hole or to Manticore."

"If it was Nulti or Slaney in that chair," ban Wyvald added, "such considerations would not be provided."

Straightening up and returning to her perch on the side of ban Wyvald's desk—which came to Ungrilig as something of a relief, both for his fear and his nose—Tresyllione said, "It also helps that Hanna spoke well of you."

That brought Ungrilig up short. "She did?"

Tresyllione nodded. "She told us that you had stopped gambling and that you were working to pay off your debts. Maybe remember that the next time you decide to call her a bitch."

Ungrilig winced. "I'm sorry about that, I just—"

"Was caught off guard because we found out you're a bribe-taking piece of troll dung?" Tresyllione asked. The half-elf was relentless.

Unable to say anything else that wouldn't sound pathetic, Ungrilig simply replied, "Yes. That."

Putting a hand on Ungrilig's shoulder, ban Wyvald said, "We'll talk to the captain. We can't promise anything, but we will try. But even if we can't get you your pension, I'm afraid that putting in your retirement papers is going to have to happen. Otherwise, we'll have no choice but to arrest you."

Nodding, Ungrilig said, "I understand, Lieutenant. Thank you. But I'm afraid that the only thing I can give you with regards to the gang that murdered Tuchera is the ringleader. I never met any of the other three, and I only saw them when they were wearing those hobgoblin masks. And I don't know where he lives or anything like that. But I can tell you his name: Crellin Quolt."

ELEVEN

"I CAN'T BELIEVE THAT'S HOW UNGRILIG, OF ALL PEOPLE, WOUND UP."

Torin sighed at Danthres's latest outburst as they worked their way back to New Barlin. She'd been going on about Ungrilig since they left the castle, having told Sergeant Jonas to get the word out to all the precincts that they wanted Crellin Quolt for questioning. Ungrilig hadn't known Quolt's address, and only provided the most general description, but at least they had a name.

"He's still a good man, Danthres. Just got led down the wrong path. We've seen it before—gambling can make a person irrational."

"That's certainly true. I would never have called Ungrilig irrational before today, certainly." Danthres shook her head as they turned down Boulder Pass. "If it was almost anyone else..." She trailed off.

"I never really got to know him that well. I mean, I've encountered him, obviously, at crime scenes and such, but you worked with him."

Danthres nodded. "The first few months in Goblin were a nightmare. I was still learning on the job, and since Captain Brisban didn't want me in the Guard, he did everything he could to make me fail."

Torin knew this much, at least. Most rookies were assigned to Unicorn or Gryphon until they got some experience. The slums of Goblin were reserved for the grizzled veterans. And also for half-elves whom the captain—Osric's predecessor—didn't want there.

"Most of the other guards knew what Brisban wanted, and so they gave me shit. And a lot of them were drooling imbeciles like Nulti and Slaney and Ganzar."

While Nulti and Slaney were still with the Guard—Nulti was still a guard in Goblin after all these years—the third was a name Torin didn't recognize. "Who's Ganzar?"

"The sergeant in charge of Goblin when I signed on. After Brisban died, Osric fired him after a week when it was discovered that he was letting prisoners go if they paid him a copper."

Torin regarded his partner dubiously as they walked past the boulder and went onto Albin Way. "'It was discovered,' was it?"

Danthres smiled viciously. "Modesty prevents me from naming the guard in question who turned him in." The smile fell. "Truly, enlightened self-interest prevented me from reporting publicly. I let Osric know, but anonymously. I didn't tell him it was me until two years after I made lieutenant."

"Was he surprised?"

"Not really. He insisted that he was sure it was me all along, though I'm not *entirely* sure I believed him. Osric always did like to seem smarter than he was."

Torin, who'd served with Osric in the war before serving under him in the Guard, silently agreed with that.

"In any case, Ganzar was always making sure that all the guards in Goblin did what they could to sabotage me. Ungrilig, though, never did that. He treated me like a colleague instead of a pain in the ass to be removed from the Guard as quickly as possible."

"Well, Captain Dru promised to talk to his lordship about it, and we'll see what happens. In the meantime, I'm far more interested in why Gedling was singled out by name—and why Tuchera got killed in his place."

"As am I."

They turned onto Central Way and first tried Gedling's residence once again. There continued to be no answer, nor any signs of life when they peered inside.

"I have a suggestion that you're not going to like," Torin said as they went to Tuchera's residence next door.

With a due sense of mock-dread, Danthres said, "All right."

"We should have Phoenix post a guard on Gedling's house. The spot-checks obviously aren't working, since he hasn't turned up, plus now that we know he was the specific target all along, they may choose to go after him again. His life is in danger, so we should watch his home."

"Why wouldn't I like— Oh." Realization dawned on Danthres's face. "That means we have to talk to Sergeant Shitbrain."

Grinning, Torin said, "Took to that nickname rather quickly, didn't you? If it makes you feel any better, I can go ask him and leave you out of it."

"He doesn't like you that much, either."

"Yes, but I don't *actually* wish to club him over the head with a blacksmith's hammer, unlike you."

Putting a hand to her chest, right over the gryphon crest on her leather armor, Danthres said, "I would never do such a thing! I respect blacksmith's hammers far too much to risk getting blood on them…"

Torin snorted his amusement, and then knocked on the Tuchera door.

He heard a good deal of coughing on the other side of the door, which meant that Migda was home, but she didn't answer the door until after she was done with her coughing fit.

"My apologies, Lieutenant."

"There is absolutely no need for you to apologize for something that it out of your control, ma'am," Torin said.

"That's very kind of you to say," she said, "but yours is a unique reaction. Most people view my coughs as a rude interruption to a conversation. It's gotten to the point where I prefer to avoid talking with any of my fellow citizens. Not," she added with a tone of bitterness, "that too many of them are going out of their way to talk to me. Prior to today, anyhow. Today, it's been all condolences and apologies for Tuchera's death, all from people who barely acknowledged our existence two days ago."

"We won't take up too much of your time, we simply wish to ask you about Gedling."

"What about him?"

"How well do you know him?"

Migda shrugged. "To say hello to, really. Tuchera spoke to him more than I did, and we would converse about meaningless topics—or subjects relating to our homes. Privy cleaning, purchasing foodstuffs, that sort of thing. I didn't even know he was a landscaper until he asked Tuchera to take his shift."

Danthres asked, "How did he seem when he asked Tuchera to do that?"

Putting a finger to her chin, Migda seemed to be thinking over her answer. "Funny you should ask, Lieutenant—he seemed a bit skittish. And nervous. And, more to the point, he didn't seem to be at all sick.

I'm perhaps a bit more sensitive to it, given my own condition, but he didn't appear to be ill in any way. We didn't question it, as it was a job, and in Tuchera's field on top of that. We were hardly about to look a gift orc in the mouth."

"Indeed," Torin said. "And you haven't seen him at all?"

"No, not since he asked Tuchera to take his shift." Migda gave a derisive chuckle. "In fact, he's the only neighbor who *hasn't* come by to offer condolences. Which is pretty awful of him, since it was his damn fault that Tuchera was attacked."

More than you think. Torin did not say that part out loud, however. "Thank you, ma'am. We'll leave you to it. If you do see Gedling at any point, please inform a guard."

"We'll also be posting a guard to watch his house next door," Danthres said, "so don't be alarmed by that."

"That's a bit extreme, isn't it?"

Torin hesitated before answering Migda's question. "He's a person of interest in this murder and we've yet to speak to him. Indeed, no one has seen him since before your husband was killed. So we're going to have to keep an eye on his home in the hopes that he returns."

"I suppose that makes sense." Migda then let loose with a brutal cough.

Torin stood awkwardly in the doorway, exchanging a glance with Danthres, who just shrugged.

Once she was done coughing, Torin held up a hand. "Please don't apologize, ma'am. We'll be on our way."

With that, he turned to leave, Danthres quickly following.

Minutes later, they walked into Phoenix Precinct only to find no one sitting at the desk. Various guards were moving about, a susurrus of noise hovering over the entire large room.

Bellowing at the top of her lungs, Danthres cried out, *"Has anyone seen Sergeant Slaney?"*

That got the place to quiet down, and everyone turned to stare at her.

"I'm right 'ere," came a voice from behind them.

Turning, Torin saw that Slaney was entering from outside, carrying several parchments. "We need you—" Torin started.

"I don't give a troll's ass whatcha 'need,' red. I gotta precinct t'run, I ain't got time f'r—"

Danthres stepped forward to loom over Slaney in much the same way she had over Ungrilig, though Slaney was standing, and taller than the dwarf—and also wasn't particularly intimidated. "*I* don't give a troll's ass about your job, Slaney. We need you to put a guard on Gedling's house on Central Way."

"Why for?"

Torin said, "We need to question him. He was the intended target of our murder victim."

"What, that *bahrlan* that got hisself killed near th'boulder?"

"Yes," Danthres said through clenched teeth, "the *refugee* who was killed. The people who beat him to death were supposed to beat Gedling to death. But he called in sick to work, and Tuchera went instead."

"Why should I give a shit? I mean, who cares which *bahrlan* they killed?"

"For one thing," Torin said, "once they realized they killed the wrong person, they may try again. Gedling's life is in danger."

"Look, I'll try, but I got shit t'do 'ere, an' I ain't got time f'r babysittin' some 'ouse."

"Well," Danthres said, "I'm certainly going to have a great deal to tell Lady Meerka when I meet with her at the end of the shift."

"As will Captain Dru when he meets with Lord Doval next."

Slaney was now moving back to his desk, and he dropped the parchments unceremoniously onto its already-crowded surface. He glared at the two detectives. "Don' gimme that. No way you're meetin' with no Lady Meerka."

"Try me." Danthres leaned forward, palms flat on Slaney's desk. "I've had the lady's ear for over a year now, and she trusts my judgment."

"And the captain has breakfast with his lordship once a week."

"So please," Danthres said, "continue to inform us how you won't follow our direct orders, *Sergeant*."

"Look, I—"

Jared walked over, having been watching this tableau with amusement. "I'll take care of it, Sarge."

"What?" Slaney looked completely lost.

"I'll keep an eye on Gedling's place. I already kicked that drunk, so I'm free."

"Why'dja kick the drunk?"

Jared just stared at him. "You *told* me to."

"I did? Shit." Slaney waved his hand in Danthres's face. "Fine, the hell with it, go 'head, Jared, watch that *bahrlan*'s house. I don't give a shit." Slaney walked out from behind the desk and went to the staircase.

"Thank you," Torin said to Jared.

"Gets me outta the precinct house and away from Sergeant Shitbrain, so it's *really* no problem, Lieutenants."

Danthres grinned. "That's the spirit, Jared."

As the three of them moved to the exit, Jared asked in a whisper, "Hey, is it true what I heard, that Ungrilig's retiring?"

Neutrally, Torin said, "That's the rumor."

"Too bad, but prob'ly for the best. Poor bastard can barely walk. Dunno why he didn't put in his papers when Blayk offered it last year."

"It's a mystery," Torin said blandly.

Jared went off toward Central Way, while Torin and Danthres continued on Albin Way toward the boulder.

"You realize," Danthres said, "that word will get out about Ungrilig soon enough."

"No doubt, but I see no reason to slander him unnecessarily. As you said, he was a good guard once. Better he be remembered that way."

"Somebody should…" Danthres muttered.

TWELVE

As Captain Dru approached Lord Doval's office, his lordship's
secretary, an elderly gnome woman named Taja, looked up and smiled
broadly at his approach.

"Captain, it's so good to see you!"

"Thanks, Taja. Rupert came by, said he could talk t'me now?"
Rupert was one of the pageboys, who had just been sent to the eastern
wing of the castle to inform Dru that Lord Doval had a few minutes to
meet with him.

"Yes, but only for a few minutes, I'm afraid. He's to meet with
Madam Brigit to discuss the arrangement for Sir Louff's hundredth
birthday party."

Dru blinked. Humans rarely made it to the century mark. "He's a
hundred?"

Nodding, Taja said, "Next week. We're all very impressed, especially given how appalling his eating habits are."

With a chuckle, Dru said, "Well, tell him happy birthday from me
when you see 'im next."

"Oh, I won't be seeing him. He's long since retired from public
service, and the only time he ever even leaves his mansion to come to
the castle is when there's a state dinner of some sort, and he doesn't
even always make those."

"Pretty sure he'll rouse himself f'this one," Dru said dryly.

"I would think. Nevertheless, secretaries are not permitted to attend
such rarefied functions."

"From what I've heard 'bout those dinners, you're prob'ly better
off."

"No doubt. In any case, I will likely barge into your meeting in about
ten minutes to take him away, so be brief, please?"

"I'll do my best." Dru grinned encouragingly and then walked past her desk into Doval's office.

Looking up from some slates he was reading, Doval said, "Ah, Captain, good to see you. Please, have a seat."

"Sorry for bugging you in the middle of the day like this, m'lord," Dru said as he sat down in the guest chair, "but this couldn't wait 'til the end'a the week."

"Quite all right." Leaning forward, he said in a stage whisper, "I'll take anything to delay having to meet with Madam Brigit. The woman is simply *exhausting*."

Dru kept a straight face — upper-class folks were fine with making fun of each other, less so with the lower classes doing it — and said, "Well, I won't take too long — don't wanna make Taja pissed at me."

"A state of affairs we all prefer, believe me. So, what is so urgent?"

"Two things. One is something I gotta ask: did you, or anybody else, authorize a company called Ankh Security to work Jorbin's Way?"

"Ankh Security?" Doval frowned with what Dru saw as a complete lack of recognition. Then, to prove it, he continued: "I've never heard of them."

"It's a company that got put together by Rob Wirrn. Used t'be a guard, he's one'a the ones your brother gave early retirement to."

Doval shook his head. "I know nothing of this, I'm afraid. What is it they're doing?"

"Protectin' folks down Jorbin's Way, supposedly. Except from what Aleta an' Dannee've been able t'figure, they're shakin' people down. Chargin' protection money, an' trashin' places that don't pay it."

"It's a fascinating notion, though I would think that's what the Castle Guard is for, yes? Minus the extortion, that is."

"Yeah. Y'wanna know what I think?"

"Absolutely."

"I think Wirrn an' some'a his guard buddies're usin' this as an excuse to make some extra coin. Everyone's all worried with all the refugees, an' 'specially with all the attacks on 'em." Dru took a breath. "If they ain't sanctioned by the castle, then I'd like your lordship's permission to shut 'em down."

"Absolutely. I've nothing against free enterprise, but I would say that this is stepping on the Castle Guard's mandate at best, and at worst is using the guise of security to intimidate and extort the populace."

Dru loved the way his lordship could say the exact same thing he did, only with completely different—and fancier—words. "Sounds good t'me."

"And the second thing?"

Now Dru sighed. Shutting down Wirrn's little gang of thugs was one thing, but he was dreading this part. "It's about another guard that your brother tried to talk into early retirement. We got a guard named Ungrilig who used t'have a gamblin' problem. He's over that, but he's still in debt up past his eyeballs."

Doval raised an eyebrow. "Past his eyeballs? I was under the impression that the saying was 'up to his eyeballs'."

Unable to help grinning, Dru said, "He's a dwarf, I figured 'up to his eyeballs' wouldn't seem like much."

"Fair enough. Go on."

"He took money from a buncha shitbrains who've been goin' around in hobgoblin masks beatin' up on refugees. He's been lookin' the other way when they attack folks near the boulder."

"Boulder?" Doval squinted in confusion as he asked the question.

That brought Dru up short. He'd walked past the boulder with his lordship twice just a few months ago when they opened Phoenix Precinct. "Where Boulder Pass meets Albin Way, m'lord."

"Oh, yes, right. I understand that boulder is all that's left of the rock creature that tried to kill Helsek Gam a thousand years ago."

That, too, surprised Dru. "Really? I always though it was a corner-stone for the original castle before they built this one. Well, anyhow, these mask-wearing shitbrains killed a man, an' Ungrilig's cooperatin' with us to get 'em. He's agreed t'retire, like Lord Blayk offered 'im last year, an' I'd like t'do that without bringin' 'im up on charges. Just let 'im take his pension and retire in peace. No sense in bringin' a guard 'fore the magistrate, 'specially one like Ungrilig. He's been a *real* good guard, mostly."

Doval rubbed his chin. "That 'mostly' caveat is rather a large one, Captain, seeing as how his mendacity led to a murder."

"He didn't know that, he thought they were just gonna rough some-one up."

"That's only a mild improvement." Doval sighed. "Still, I'd rather spare us the embarrassment of putting a guard before the magistrate. As long as this Ungrilig is no longer working for the Castle Guard, that will be sufficient. But I will not allow him to take the deal my brother offered him. I assume he's close to but not at twenty-five years?"

Dru nodded. All the people Blayk offered early retirement to were guards who were not at twenty-five years yet, but they were offered that much larger pension as an incentive.

"He may retire with his ten-year pension only."

Having expected that his lordship would deny Ungrilig any kind of pension, Dru was relieved to hear this. "That'd be perfect, m'lord, thank you."

"And you say he's cooperating with regard to these mendicants?"

"Yeah, he is. Gave us the name'a the ringleader."

"Good." Doval rubbed his chin a bit more. "Captain, do you think that this Rob Wirrn person with his security force has a point?"

"Whaddaya mean, m'lord?"

"Well, people *are* feeling insecure, and not without reason. Perhaps it would be wise to do another recruiting drive, add some guards to Dragon, Goblin, and Mermaid strictly for security. Simply to plant the flag, as it were, make more of a Castle Guard presence in areas that have been troublesome."

"I ain't gonna object t'more guards," Dru said slowly, "but what I really need is two more detectives."

Abashedly, Doval said, "Rebuke taken, Captain—I've yet to have a moment to speak to my mother on that particular subject."

"S'all right, m'lord," Dru said, as if it could be anything other than all right. "But I'm all for whatever you wanna do t'make us more efficient."

Taja came into the office, then. "Apologies, m'lord, but Madam Brigit is waiting, and—"

Holding up a hand and rising to his feet, Doval said, "Yes, yes, absolutely, Taja, I'll head over there now. Assuming the captain is finished?"

Dru had also gotten up and quickly said, "No, no, that's it. I mean, yeah, there's other stuff, but we can cover it at breakfast in a couple days."

Clapping his hands, Doval said, "Excellent. See you then, Captain."

THIRTEEN

Jak Reesh was approaching the door to the apartment building where Torin lived as the latter was exiting to go to work.

"Oh, Wiate's fingernail!" Jak exclaimed as he saw that Torin was fully armored up. "I thought for sure you'd be running late like always, and I'd catch you."

Torin considered explaining that he left on time precisely because Jak wasn't there, but decided that trying to guilt his lover in that manner would be unworthy of him. So instead, he screwed a smile onto his face and said, "You are obviously *quite* special, Jak, as you have arrived on one of the vanishingly rare occasions when I'm likely to arrive at work on time."

Shaking his head and laughing, Jak put both his hands on Torin's shoulders and stared into his eyes. "My timing remains terrible. I actually got a break on my overnight job, so I thought I'd be able to come wake you up, at least."

"Alas." Torin cupped his hands on Jak's wrists. "Perhaps tonight we can truly *see* each other? And then you can explain to me the significance of Wiate's fingernail—and perhaps tell me which fingernail in particular is referred to in that oath?"

Jak smiled, which broadened Torin's. He loved it when Jak swore on some random body part of the god Wiate, and over the past few months, Torin had been collecting Jak's explanations about the importance of whatever body part he'd chosen with the same joy and pleasure with which he'd spent the last decade collecting stories about the boulder.

"It's the middle fingernail of his right hand, and as for tonight, I'm not sure. My new boss got called away, so I don't know what my schedule is. But if I'm still free, I'll wait for you here tonight, all right?"

Torin grinned. "Excellent!" He leaned forward and kissed Jak. "I hope to see you later, then."

With a spring in his step, he proceeded down toward Meerka Way and thence to the castle.

He arrived at the squadroom at the same time as Jonas—something that had never happened in the years since Jonas took over as sergeant—which meant that he got first crack at the pastries that Jonas's wife made every morning for the squadroom. His recent bout of arriving on time had meant that, at least, of late he'd been able to eat the pastries while they were still warm, but there was always *someone* who arrived before him, even lately.

"Your wife remains a wizard in the kitchen, Jonas," Torin said.

"I'll be sure to tell her you said so," the sergeant said with a short nod. Then he departed the pantry.

He passed Danthres on the way out. She came in the pantry as Torin was wiping flakes out of his goatée. As soon as she caught sight of Torin, she frowned. "All right, what's wrong?"

"Why do you think something's wrong?" he asked with a rakish grin.

"Because you're here on time, but you're also in a good mood."

"Jak came by just as I was leaving—terrible timing, as it turned out, though he assumed I'd still be in bed at half-six."

As she grabbed a pastry, Danthres said, "A reasonable assumption for him to make, all things considered."

"True."

Jonas stuck his head back into the pantry. "Torin, Danthres, Frida from the youth squad just came in, she said they found Crellin Quolt."

"Finally," Danthres said with a full mouth.

Torin regarded his partner with a raised eyebrow. "Danthres, we only put his name out yesterday. Sometimes it takes weeks before we find someone."

Shrugging, she said, "I'm impatient, what can I tell you?"

Snorting, Torin asked Jonas, "Where is Quolt?"

"Garis and Micah are bringing him in."

"Is Frida still about?" Torin asked.

Jonas glanced behind him. "Not sure. If not, I'm sure I can grab someone else—or send a guard, why what do you need?"

"Ungrilig. We need to verify that Quolt is the one who paid him off."

Shaking his head, Jonas said, "We don't need Frida for that—Ungrilig's here in the castle, filling out his retirement paperwork. I'll send someone to Sir Rommett's office to fetch him."

Danthres said, "Keep him in the squadroom until we're ready for him."

Nodding, Jonas left the pantry. Torin and Danthres both ate one more pastry each, and then went to their desks to await the arrival of their prisoner.

Manfred, Kellan, Aleta, and Dannee all came in while they were waiting. The former three all felt the need to comment on Torin beating them in this morning.

"Torin? Is that you?" from Manfred.

"Wow, the time chimes must be malfunctioning—if I'm here after Torin, I must be an hour late!" from Kellan.

"I think I read a prophecy once, back home, that stated that Torin arriving on time for work more than three times in a week is a sign of the end of the world..." from Aleta.

Torin looked across his desk to Danthres and sighed. "I suppose eleven years of tardiness has earned me this abuse."

"Oh, no, it's earned you a lot *more* abuse, but they all like and respect you, so they're taking it easy." Danthres chuckled, then her face grew a bit more serious. "I am rather surprised to learn that Aleta reads prophecies."

Dannee then said, "I don't think it's very nice to tease you about it."

"Thank you, Dannee," Torin said with a bow of his head to his colleague.

Aleta said, "My parents were devotees of Olthrathish, so I had memorized all nineteen prophecies by the time I was five."

Eyes widening, Danthres said, "I didn't think anyone still worshipped Olthranthish. Especially after the Elf Queen abolished all religions except worship of her."

"There were a few, though they were all—" Aleta hesitated. "They were all taken care of before too long."

Torin read between the lines there. "Your parents were killed?"

Aleta nodded. "I was seven when the Shranlaseth came for them. Because I was so young, I was spared, and I was taken in by the Shranlaseth."

Now Torin's eyes were the ones widening. "You started training with them at age seven?"

"Not at first—the Elf Queen ran an orphanage and I was raised there. But when I was old enough to hold a weapon, I was informed that I would be trained to become Shranlaseth, which was required in order to do penance for my parents' blasphemy."

"So they forced you?" Danthres asked.

Aleta nodded.

Danthres looked to Torin as if she wanted to ask more questions, but then Garis, Micah, and a skinny, unassuming-looking human entered the squadroom.

Torin got to his feet immediately. "This must be Crellin Quolt?"

"Yeah," Garis said.

Quolt himself spoke up. "The, um, the guards here, they said you, ah, wanted to talk to me about an assault? I, um, I don't know anything about any kind of, ah, assaulting, I'm afraid."

"Your name came up in our inquiries." Torin pointed at the door to one of the interrogation rooms. "If you could just wait in there, we'll try not to take up too much of your time."

"Um, I guess so." Quolt turned and walked quietly into the interrogation room.

Danthres, still seated, looked up at Garis and Micah. "Where'd you find him?"

Micah said, "Y'know that new breakfast stall on Stone Path? We was gettin' some breakfast there. Well, we was on line, anyhow. Way it works is, you order, give 'em your name, and they call you up when it's ready. So me an' Garis is on line, an' then we hear 'em call out Quolt. Soon's he walks up to get his sausage roll, we grab him."

"We said to him that he was wanted for questioning," Garis said. "That's okay, right?"

Now, Danthres finally got to her feet. "Yes, better to keep him at ease and think he's a witness rather than a suspect. Did you get his address?"

"Yeah," Micah said, "he's got a room on Stone Path right down the road from the breakfast stall."

"We need you to go there and search his room. Look for a hobgoblin mask."

The two guards exchanged looks. "We can do that, yeah," Micah started.

"The thing is," Garis said hesitantly, "we never got our breakfast. And Micah tells me that Sergeant Jonas's wife makes excellent pastries."

Indicating the way to the pantry, Torin said, "Help yourselves before you head back to Stone Path."

Both guards grinned hungrily. "Toldja," Micah said as they beelined for the pantry. "Only thing I miss 'bout bein' assigned to Gryphon is these pastries."

"The *only* thing?" Garis asked incredulously. "You complain *every single day* about how much more walking you have to do since you transferred to Dragon."

The rest of their banter was lost to their entering the pantry. Torin turned to his partner.

Danthres was back to staring at Aleta.

"We can finish talking to her later," Torin said.

Shaking her head as if to clear it, Danthres said, "You're right, of course. Sorry, I just—" She blew out a breath. "We should treat him like a regular witness, the same way Garis and Micah did, see if we can trip him up. Once Ungrilig gets here, we can have him identify him, and whatever those two find in his place after they stuff their faces will top everything off nicely."

"Agreed."

As they entered the interrogation room, Torin saw that Quolt was picking at the wood on the table while sitting in one of the two stools on the door side. The room had no windows, the only illumination provided by a single lantern.

"Please, sir," Torin said as he entered, "if you could take the seat on the other side of the table?"

"What difference does it make?"

"It simply makes the questioning easier if both of us are on the same side of the table," Torin lied. Well, it wasn't a complete lie, what he said was true as far as it went, but also suspects were generally kept in a place where there was a table and two guards between them and the only exit.

Also the chair on the other side of the table was less comfortable…

"Fine, I suppose." Quolt got up and sat on the other side.

Torin sat in one of the two chairs on the door side. "I'm Lieutenant Torin ban Wyvald, and this is my partner, Lieutenant Danthres Tresyllione. We're investigating several attacks that have been made on refugees of late, including one that ended in murder."

"Refugees?" Quolt sounded confused.

Danthres finally spoke as she took her seat next to Torin. "People who came here from Barlin after the fire."

"Oh, *bahrlans*. Right. Yes, I've heard about some of those people being attacked. It's fine with me."

"Excuse me?" Danthres said in a dangerous tone.

Quolt seemed utterly unintimidated, which was unusual for people on the other side of that tone of hers. "They're *bahrlans*. Who cares if they get beat up a little? Serves them right for coming here and taking our jobs and our food."

"To answer your question," Torin said before Danthres could react to that, "who cares is us. The lord and lady's laws specifically prohibit assault and battery—and murder."

"Of Cliff's End citizens, sure, but *bahrlans*? They're not from here."

Tightly, Danthres said, "Many people who live in Cliff's End aren't 'from here.' In fact, of the six lieutenants in the Castle Guard, only two were born here. Torin was born in Myverin, Lieutenant lothLathna was born in elf country, Lieutenant Oclee was born in Barlin—before the fire, mind you—and I came here from Sorlin."

"Came here?" Quolt's head tilted to the side. "You weren't born in—what did you say, Sorlin? Never heard of the place."

Danthres had no idea where she was born—her mother brought her to Sorlin when she was an infant and died shortly thereafter—though her maternal family was from Treemark. However, she also made it a policy never to answer questions in this room, so instead she simply said, "The point is, a good percentage of the population of the city-state isn't originally from here. And the lord and lady's laws apply to everyone in the demesne regardless of where they were born."

"Which is why," Torin said, "when someone is killed, we investigate, and if we find the perpetrator, they are brought before the magistrate and, in all likelihood, hanged."

"Hanged!" For the first time, Quolt reacted in a manner other than blasé. "That's a little extreme, isn't it?"

"For murder?" Danthres scoffed. "It's appropriate. If you take a life, then your life should be taken in exchange."

"I guess. So why am I here, exactly?"

"According to a witness we've interviewed, you were present at more than one of the assaults."

"Well, that witness is lying. I've never seen any *bahrlans* getting beat up. Mind you, I wouldn't mind if I did, but—" Quolt folded his arms over his chest. "If that's all?"

"I doubt the witness is lying," Torin said, "as he's a guard in good standing. Ungrilig has been serving in the Castle Guard for nearly two-and-a-half decades."

"First of all," Quolt said exasperatedly, "Ungrilig is a useless old troll who can barely walk. Second of all, he didn't see *anything*, if he knows what's good for him."

"And what do you mean by that?" Torin asked blandly.

Belatedly realizing that he'd given it away, as it were, Quolt quickly backtracked. "I mean—he couldn't—that is—" He coughed. "Look, everyone knows that Ungrilig takes bribes. He bets on hobgoblin races and the like. You can't trust him."

"Oh, I think we can," Danthres said. "You see, we caught him taking bribes and betting on hobgoblin races and the like. He gave you up as part of the deal to keep him from being arrested."

"So if he was lying," Torin said, "he goes to jail. Therefore, he's motivated to tell us the truth."

"Look, I didn't see anything, all right? And even if I did, who cares? It's just some *bahrlan*. We're better off without Gedling taking jobs away from us!"

Danthres frowned. "I'm sorry, who's Gedling?"

That seemed to bring Quolt up short. "Gedling's the one who was killed, right? You said so."

"Actually," Torin said, "we never said the name of the victim—which was *not* Gedling, it was Tuchera."

"That can't be! They told us to get the *bahrlan* working for the Fansarris! Gedling was working for—"

And then Quolt closed his eyes and sighed.

Torin grinned. It was always amusing when the suspects incriminated themselves. "And who is 'they' who told you this?"

Folding his arms and sitting defiantly, Quolt said, "I'm not saying another word."

"Fine." Danthres got up and walked to the door and opened it. "Come on in," she called out.

Ungrilig entered the room. "That's him. He's the one."

Now Quolt got to his feet, shouting. "You stupid old bastard! We *paid* you to keep your mouth shut!"

Ungrilig pointed an accusing finger at Quolt. "No, you paid me to look the other way when you beat some *bahrlans* up. Not kill them."

"And you didn't even kill the right person," Danthres said.

"Yeah." Quolt sighed, looked down at the floor, then looked up at the detectives. "This Tuchera guy—he's a *bahrlan*, too, yes?"

"He's a refugee from Barlin, yes," Torin said slowly.

"Then we still got rid of one of those leeches." He sat back down and smiled. "So we still did our jobs."

Jonas knocked on the interrogation room door and then came in. "One of the youth squad just came with a message: Micah and Garis found a red hobgoblin mask in Quolt's room."

Torin turned to look at Quolt. "Well. It seems that's that."

"What's what?"

"Crellin Quolt," Torin said formally, "you are under arrest for the murder of Tuchera."

"Really? Well, fine whatever, do what you want. But I don't care what you say, I'm not going to be hanged."

"Oh you don't think so?" Danthres asked.

"I know so."

"The only way you're going to avoid being hanged," Danthres said, "is if you give up your three cohorts."

"No chance," Quolt said. "I won't give up my friends. And I won't be hanged, either. You watch—I'm doing a public service, not a crime."

FOURTEEN

DANNEE OCLY WALKED ALONGSIDE HER PARTNER AS THEY APPROACHED THE
tiny storefront on Meerka Way that turned out to be the headquarters of
Ankh Security.

"I'm looking forward to this," she'd said to Aleta lothLathna as
they'd first left the castle prepared to follow Lord Doval's instructions,
as relayed by Captain Dru, to shut Ankh Security down. "It's bad
enough when people commit criminal acts, but to do it while pretending to be helping people? That's just mean."

Inside was a tiny space with three chairs and one desk. They walked
in to see an elf sitting in one of the chairs, with two people on either side
holding him down.

"You cannot hold me here!" the elf in the chair was shouting. "I'm
innocent of any wrongdoing!"

Sitting behind the desk was a tall human with white hair, whom
Dannee recognized from the one time she'd met him as Rob Wirrn.
"Be silent, over there."

Upon sighting the two lieutenants entering, the elf tried to get up,
but the two guards shoved him back into the chair. "Lieutenants! I'm
being held here against my will!"

Wirrn also noticed their entrance. "Ah, greetings—it's Lieutenants
lothLathna and Ocly, yes?"

"Yes," Aleta said, "and you're Rob Wirrn of Ankh Security."

"I'm glad you're here, actually. You're saving me a trip to Dragon
Precinct." Wirrn pointed at the elf. "This Ear burned down a vegetable
stand."

Dannee sneered at him. "You shouldn't be glad we're here."

Wirrn recoiled as if Dannee had struck him. "What's going on?"

Aleta removed the scroll that she had rolled up and placed in her belt and placed it on Wirrn's desk. "This is an official order form the lord and lady shutting Ankh Security down."

"What?" Wirrn got to his feet, his face now twisted in a rictus of anger. "How can you do this?"

"Very easily," Dannee said. "I'm sorry you won't get to intimidate people and extort money from them."

"We don't extort anything!"

Aleta gazed witheringly at Wirrn. "Please. You charge protection money. That's what criminals do."

"I don't have that many people. I have to pick and choose who we provide protection to because I can't cover all the territory. And before you say anything, neither can the Castle Guard. That's why I started Ankh in the first place."

Dannee stared at him incredulously. "How can you say that? Hallam didn't pay the protection money, and you targeted his stall. Jora Kenspal *did* pay her protection money, and she still got vandalized."

"We didn't target Hallam, he did," Wirrn said, pointing at the elf they had in custody, "but we weren't able to protect him, either, because — as I *said* — we don't have enough people." He sighed. "As for Jora, I feel terrible about that. Someone was supposed to be keeping an eye on her booth, but he was looking at the wrong one. I had to sack him, so now we're even *more* short-handed. But we have some leads on who did it — it's four people, who were all wearing different colored hobgoblin masks."

"We're already aware of that," Dannee said, "from Boneen's peel-back of the crime scene."

"That's good that the M.E. confirmed it! We're trying to track them down, but as I keep telling you, we're kind of short-handed. But we're —"

"You're now *completely* short-handed," Aleta said, "as you're shut down. And we're arresting you for extortion."

"That's insane!" Wirrn walked around the desk to face Aleta. "When a blacksmith charges money to shoe a horse, is that extortion? When you give a jeweler gold for a necklace, is the jeweler committing an act of extortion?"

"Of course not," Dannee said, "but this is different."

Pointing an accusatory finger at Dannee, Wirrn said, "No, it isn't! We're charging money for our services, just like *everyone else!*"

In a very even tone, Aleta said, "Please lower your voice, Mr. Wirrn."

Wirrn turned to face Aleta again, and started to speak. Then he saw the look on her face, and he wilted a bit.

Dannee wilted too—her partner used to be part of the elven elite special forces, and she was an incredibly dangerous individual. Aleta scared her to death, truth be told, and if she hadn't spent so much time with her being normal—everyday work, and off-duty at the Chain—Danee would do everything she could to stay away from her. But she had her violent tendencies under complete control, and they only came out when required for duty, which Dannee appreciated.

"Look, I have to pay my people, right? I was able to start up the business using my savings, but my pension is just enough to pay my own living expenses. The fees we charge for our services are to maintain the business—plus the emergency fund for the merchants."

"Emergency fund?" Dannee asked.

"We put aside fifteen percent of all our fees—what you keep insisting on calling 'protection money'—into an account at the Cliff's End Bank. Look, I can prove all this." He walked around to a corner of the office, which had a shelf filled with scrolls.

He removed one and brought it to the table, unrolling it. It was filled with names and numbers.

Aleta stared at it for but a second, and said, "You expect this gibberish to exonerate you?"

But Dannee was studying it very closely. The top of the scroll was labelled as income, and had several names, which she recognized as merchants down Jorbin's Way. The numbers next to them were all the same amounts, paid weekly, according to the dates atop those parts of the chart. The bottom of the scroll was labelled as expenses, and had another list of names, one or two of which she recognized as former guards, as well as rent, supplies, and finally a listing for the emergency fund he'd mentioned.

What's more, in each column, the amount given to the emergency fund was fifteen percent of what they took in from the amounts in the income columns.

"Um, Aleta?"

"What?"

Dannee was very reluctant to say what she was about to say, but she simply had to. "I don't know if it *exonerates* him, but—well, this chart does gibe with what he said."

"This all makes sense to you?"

Nodding, Dannee said, "I used to keep the books for my father's architecture business. This is what the ledger should look like, based on what he said."

"Numbers on a scroll aren't proof of anything," Aleta said. "And the fact that both Hallam and the Kenspals weren't at all protected shows that they're not really getting their money's worth."

"We're still new," Wirrn said, "but we're getting better. Besides, some of the merchants don't like to deal with the Castle Guard, you know that as well as I do, Aleta. The other day, two merchants got into a fight, but they didn't want to report it to anyone from Dragon Precinct because that would shut down both their stalls while it was settled—they'd lose too much money."

"If people won't report crimes to the Castle Guard, they don't deserve justice," Aleta said. "And you're operating without the lord and lady's approval, and now they've sanctioned you."

"Look, we're just trying to make things better!" Wirrn pointed at the elf they'd detained. "Hallam had stopped paying, but we captured that Ear anyhow, and we're gonna use the emergency fund to help Hallam out."

"I don't believe you," Aleta said. "I'm assuming that fifteen percent is to line your pockets. So are the salaries."

"Look, I can prove it about the bank. Come with me to Auburn Way, I'll show you the bank records."

Aleta snarled. "This is a waste of time."

"We should check," Dannee said.

Whirling on her partner, Aleta asked, "What for?"

"Look, we can still shut this place down like the captain told us, but I think we should give Mr. Wirrn a chance to prove himself. Come on, Aleta, he was one of us."

Aleta's nostrils flared in that way she did when she was annoyed about something but going to give in, which relieved Dannee.

"Fine." She turned to Wirrn. "I want you and everyone out of here."

"But—"

"Now," Aleta said in a tone that indicated very strongly that she would not repeat the instruction again, but instead apply the order with physical force.

The two employees picked the elf up out of the chair and followed Wirrn out the door.

"Lock it," Aleta said, and Wirrn quickly did so.

Aleta then affixed the shut-down order to the front door.

Dannee started to look around for one of the youth squad, but she found something better: Malva, a guard from Dragon Precinct, who was walking up Meerka Way. She signalled her.

"Hi, Dannee, Aleta. Oh, Rob, good to see you. What's all this?"

Pointing at Wirrn's two employees and the elf, Aleta said, "Take these three to Dragon. Put the elf in the hole and take statements from the other two."

"It may lead to other arrests," Dannee added.

"I doubt it," Wirrn said.

"What's going on?" Malva asked, confused. "Rob, I thought you were retired."

Wirrn held up both hands. "It's all fine. Shart and Raizo will explain everything." To those two employees, he said, "Go with Malva, answer all her questions."

One of them said, "Boss, I don't like—"

"Don't worry about it, Shart," Wirrn said. "We'll be fine. Go with Malva."

"But, Boss—"

Aleta stepped between Shart and Wirrn. "He said not to worry about it and to go with Malva. Any particular reason why you're not obeying that order?"

Shart swallowed audibly, and quietly moved off with Malva and Raizo and the elf down Meerka Way.

"There was no call for that," Wirrn said.

"There was no call to tell him that you would be fine, either," Aleta said.

Dannee said nothing, but she was biting her lip. She had been so angry before they got here, and now she was all confused.

As they walked the other way down Meerka Way toward the bank branch on Auburn Way, two people saw Wirrn and smiled.

"Hey, Rob, thanks for the help with those missing fruits!"

"Yeah, we'd have been really screwed if you hadn't helped out."

That just made Dannee feel worse.

They arrived at the Cliff's End Bank, entering just as a familiar face was walking across the floor.

"Captain Grovis!" Aleta called out.

Amilar Grovis stopped, turned, and stared in confusion at the trio who entered. Then he broke into a smile. "Goodness! Aleta! It's been ages, how are you?"

"I'm well. This is my new partner, Dannee Ocly."

Grovis walked over and inclined his head to Dannee. "A pleasure." Looking back at Aleta, he said, "And it's 'Mr. Grovis,' if you please, Lieutenant. I'm no longer a captain in the Castle Guard, and I was never very good at it in the first place. Or a detective, truth be told."

"So things are going well here at the bank?" Aleta asked.

"Yes, absolutely. Ah, Mr. Wirrn! Good to see you again." Grovis's face fell a bit. "Oh dear, is something wrong with Ankh's account?"

Dannee jumped on that. "Ankh Security *does* have an account here?"

"Oh, absolutely. I set it up for Mr. Wirrn here shortly after I started my job as manager. Why, is there a problem?"

"Not with the account," Wirrn said quietly.

While Dannee had never dealt directly with Grovis during his years as a detective or his few weeks as captain, she had heard about him, including that he had a face like a fish. Upon entering the bank, she hadn't understood the analogy, but right now, Grovis's face sort of went limp and his mouth hung open slightly, and then it all made sense. He looked *exactly* like a fish right now.

"Then I'm confused," Grovis said in his piscine glory, "what is the Castle Guard doing escorting our client into the bank?"

"The problem isn't with the account Cap—" Aleta stopped herself. "Mr. Grovis, the problem is with Ankh Security itself. The lord and lady have ordered that the company be shut down."

"What? That's absurd! Mr. Wirrn here is providing a valuable supplement to the Castle Guard's good work! What's more, he's helping the victims!"

"That's what he told us," Aleta said, "and I'm afraid we're going to require proof of that."

"I would be happy to provide such. Come with me." Grovis turned and headed back the opposite way he'd been walking when they came in.

Dannee followed him, as did Aleta and Wirrn, the latter saying, "I *did* tell you."

"Do yourself a favor," Aleta said quietly, "and stop talking."

Wirrn went ashen, and nodded quickly.

Grovis's office was surprisingly small. It was, however, quite neat and tidy, with scrolls organized neatly on shelves behind a wooden desk. He walked over to the shelf and ran his fingers over several before finally pulling one out. "Ah, here we are."

Turning, he spread the scroll out over the desk surface.

"What are we looking at?" Aleta asked.

"The affidavit that accompanied Mr. Wirrn's opening of the Ankh Security account. I point you to this clause." Grovis's finger landed on one paragraph.

Dannee read it aloud. "'Any withdrawals must be accompanied by a document affirming the use to which the funds will be put, and that use must be a charitable one relating to a client of the account holder, and must be approved by a representative of the Cliff's End Bank.'" She looked up at Grovis. "This means he can't withdraw from the account without your approval?"

"That is correct. And Mr. Wirrn was adamant that this affidavit be a part of the account he set up."

"I'm not trying to extort anyone," Wirrn said, "I'm trying to provide a service."

"This is terrible," Dannee said, feeling absolutely miserable.

Grovis, for his part, was growing more cross. "I cannot believe the lord and lady would just shut Ankh down like that without consulting Mr. Wirrn—or the bank!"

Aleta put her hands on her hips. "And I can't believe that Mr. Wirrn just started a security company that steps on the Castle Guard without consulting the Castle Guard, or anyone else in the western wing of the castle. The reason why Lord Doval signed and sealed the shut-down order was because he didn't know *anything* about Ankh Security, and none of the guards in Dragon knew about it, either."

"I don't need to consult the castle to create a business," Wirrn said.

Dannee said, "But you do if you create a business that interferes with a government service. I mean—look at the prison barge! They didn't just create a prison and start putting criminals in it, they approached the castle and got a contract to take on prison services."

"Yeah, and they became part of the Castle Guard eventually," Wirrn said. "I'm not looking for that."

"Yes, it's Manticore Precinct now, but it was independent for years. So's the body shop, for that matter," Dannee said, referring to the crematorium in a cave in the Forest of Nimvale where unclaimed bodies were disposed of.

"If you wish," Grovis said, "I will have my father speak with Lord Doval on your behalf."

"Regardless," Aleta said, "the shut-down order remains intact. And I need to take you to the castle."

"Fine," Wirrn said.

Dannee hung her head. Even though she agreed with Aleta's point, she still felt terrible. It looked like Wirrn was legitimately trying to do some good down Jorbin's Way, and they'd just spoiled it. She took on this job to help people, not hurt them, and she felt like she'd just dealt a major bit of hurt to someone who did not deserve it...

FIFTEEN

Sir Rommett came into his office this morning to yet another memo from Lord Doval.

On the one hand, he understood why his lordship put his requests in writing rather than provide those requests in person via meetings, as his father Lord Albin had. There was a level of accountability that a scroll with the lord and lady's seal had that a conversation in Lord Albin's sitting room did not have.

Of course, Lord Albin's word was his bond. He never changed his mind capriciously, and on those occasions when he found the need to reverse a decision he had made, he went through detailed channels to make sure the reversal did the least amount of damage.

Lord Doval, however, seemed to be perpetually too busy to meet with Sir Rommett, and said he preferred the more direct method of sending memos. This despite the fact that he had recently started meeting on a weekly basis with Captain Dru over breakfast, which Rommett had found odd.

A part of Rommett missed the meetings with Lord Albin in the sitting room. The fire blazing, a glass of some manner of drink in both their hands as they discussed the business of the city-state. When he had met with Albin's son, it had been in Doval's office.

But another part of Rommett was grateful that he hadn't had to set foot in the sitting room since the morning he found Lord Albin's body over a year ago.

To this day, Rommett still had nightmares about that day. In fact, his most recent had been the previous night, when he'd woken up screaming after reliving the sight of Lord Albin's unmoving body in the sitting room.

Putting the awful memory to one side as best he could, he turned his focus to the memo in question. Apparently Lord Doval wished to put part of the Castle Guard's budget toward hiring two new detectives.

Prior to the fire in Barlin, Rommett would have expressed an objection to such a line item, but the way that the crime rate had spiked of late, he couldn't scrape together any kind of objection. The number of cases the detectives had had to deal with since the population increased thanks to the Barlin refugees was damaging to the detective squad's efficiency.

He was about to call for his secretary to come in to ask him to set up a meeting with Captain Dru to discuss who among the guards to promote when Bertram shoved his head in the door before Rommett could call his name.

"Uhm, excuse me, I'm sorry to interrupt, but Sir and Madam Fansarri are here to see you."

"What is it that *they* want?" Rommett asked, confused. Aside from sharing a table at state dinners, he'd had virtually no interactions with the Fansarris.

"They didn't say, just that it was urgent," Bertram said. "And Madam Fansarri said she'd go to Lady Meerka if you didn't see them right away. She also made it clear that her ladyship is a close personal friend of hers."

Rommett knew for a fact that wasn't true — if nothing else, Lady Meerka didn't really have friends so much as people she tolerated more than others, and the Fansarris were most assuredly *not* on that small list — but he also knew that the Fansarris would annoy her ladyship. They would tell Lady Meerka that Sir Rommett didn't see them, and she'd send them back to Rommett with a sternly worded instruction not to get her involved in his ridiculous business.

And so, with a heavy sigh and a due sense of dread, he told Bertram, "Show them in."

Boslin and Elmira Fansarri entered. As usual, Madam Fansarri was covered in a ton of makeup, as the family had a legendary disdain for magick that kept her from using glamours like a normal person. For his part, Sir Fansarri had shaved his head since the last time Rommett had seen him, which was likely a sop to his receding hairline.

Boslin spoke in a very quiet voice, barely opening his mouth. "Thank you for seeing us, Rommett." That, to Rommett's mind, meant that Sir Fansarri had done nothing to fix the missing tooth he'd suffered three years ago.

Luckily, his wife rarely let him get a word in, so keeping his mouth shut was fairly easy for him...

Sure enough, before Rommett could even reply to her husband and offer them a seat, Elmira said, "What are you doing about our missing landscaper?"

Blinking, Rommett asked, "Excuse me?"

"We are doing important work on our home, and we've had two landscapers go missing. First Gedling, who was sick but he should have recovered by now, and then Tuchera. We're falling behind on our work, and I want to know what the Castle Guard is *doing* about it! Lady Meerka is a close personal friend of mine, and I don't think she'll be happy to know how cavalierly you're treating this case."

The only part of Madam Fansarri's rant that rang any kind of bell with Rommett was the name Tuchera, and only because he'd just seen it in yesterday's reports from the detective squad. "I'm afraid I don't know a thing about this Gedling, but I can tell you that Tuchera won't be returning to work."

"Whyever not? Goodness, these *bahrlans* are *so* unreliable! I was told that Tuchera owned a successful landscaping company in Barlin, but I'm finding that difficult to credit, given how irresponsibly he's acting toward this opportunity."

Elmira finally took a breath, enabling Rommett to speak. "He won't be returning to work because he's been murdered."

"What?" That was Boslin, who barked out the word loudly enough that Rommett could see the gap to the left of his top front teeth.

"I don't understand," Elmira said. "Murdered?"

Rommett somehow resisted the urge to provide the definition of the verb *to murder* to Elmira. Instead, he rose to his feet, since the pair of them refused to sit down, and he was tired of looking up at them. "I'm afraid I don't know much more beyond that—the day-to-day of the Castle Guard is handled by Captain Dru, not me."

"But you're in charge," Elmira said, as if that meant he should somehow magickally know everything about every case.

"I usually don't get the details of a case until it's closed, and this investigation is still ongoing. Why don't we go to the detective squad-room and ask them? You'd get a much more satisfactory answer from them than you would from me." *And then someone else will have to put up with you*, he managed not to say out loud.

"Very well," Elmira said, "take us there."

"Bertram will be happy to—"

Putting her hands on her hips, Elmira said, "I will *not* be escorted by some flunky! I am a close personal friend of Lady Meerka's, and I will *not* have you treating my husband and I this way!"

Rommett contemplated several responses, then realized that the path of least resistance was to just escort the Fansarris to the western wing. And if he'd learned nothing else in a lifetime of being an aristocrat it was that the path of least resistance was often the safest, though not always the wisest.

He walked around his desk and exited his office, the couple trailing behind him. "Bertram, I'll be in the western wing for a bit."

Bertram just nodded, refusing to look any of the three aristocrats in the eye. Which, he admitted, was another good reason why fobbing escorting the Fansarris off on his secretary would not have been a workable notion.

"You'll be happy to know," Rommett said as they wended their way through the tapestry-covered corridors of the castle, "that the detectives in charge of Tuchera's murder investigation are Lieutenants Tresyllione and ban Wyvald."

"And why should that make me happy?" Elmira asked archly.

It shouldn't, as apparently nothing does. Once again, Rommett managed not to say those words out loud, though he thought them very aggressively. "Because they were the ones who solved the murders of Gan Brightblade and the Pirate Queen—for that matter, they're the ones who uncovered Lord Blayk's treason."

The Fansaris surprisingly had no reaction to that. Instead, there was an awkward pause, which was finally broken by Boslin saying, "I say, that's a lovely tapestry there."

"No it isn't," Elmira said. "It's tacky. They're all tacky. I miss Lord Albin's sculptures."

"I agree." Rommett was surprised to find himself concurring with Elmira on—well, anything, truly. "I was hoping that Lord Doval would restore his father's sculptures, but from what I was told, Lord Blayk donated them to a museum in Iaron, which has refused to return them."

"How very vulgar," Elmira said.

They arrived at the squadroom. Rommett saw that Lieutenants ban Wyvald and Tresyllione were present, as were Sergeant Jonas and Lieutenants Manfred and Kellan.

Rommett started to move toward ban Wyvald and Tresyllione, but Elmira made a beeline for Manfred, for some reason. "You!"

Manfred looked up and then his dark features went ashen. "Madam Fansarri."

"What are you still doing in the Castle Guard? What idiot gave you a *promotion*?"

Boslin put a hand on his wife's shoulder. "Elmira, perhaps—"

But she shrugged off her husband's hand and went over to Manfred. "Do you know that my sweet boy is *gone*? I'll *never* see my Oswalt again because of you!"

"Um—" Manfred tried to speak, but Elmira wasn't done.

"What do you have to say for yourself?"

A voice came from the other side of the squadroom. "He doesn't have t'say anything, Madam. You got a problem with one'a my detectives, talk t'me."

Rommett looked over to see Captain Dru exiting his office.

"This incompetent fool is responsible for the Brotherhood of Wizards taking my son away!"

"No, he ain't. Your son's responsible for it, 'cause he went an' studied magick on his own. Brotherhood ain't the types to take kindly t'that, an' your son's the one who opened the portal and let the hobgoblin through."

Elmira huffed and said, "Why I—I never—"

Manfred then stepped forward, which sturck Rommett as being suicidal. "Ma'am, I'm really sorry about what happened to Oswalt. If I could've stopped the brotherhood from takin' him, I would've, but—well, it's the brotherhood. There's nothing any of us could do."

Boslin quickly said, "He's right, Elmira. Let's leave him alone and talk about what we came here to discuss."

"Fine." Elmira transfrerred her glare from Manfred to Dru. "What are you doing about my missing landscaper?"

"I'm sorry?" Dru seemed confused.

Thankfully, ban Wyvald and Tresyllione stepped in. The former said, "I believe we can answer that, ma'am."

Elmira turned on the red-haired lieutenant. "Well?"

"Gedling has gone missing. We've posted a guard on his house, and we've put his description out to all the precinct sergeants. Our M.E. cast a peel-back on Gedling's house and was able to get an image of him, which he transferred to crystals. If he's sighted by any guards, we'll bring him in. In the meantime, we have suspects in the murder of Tuchera, and we're looking for them as well."

"Unfortunately," Tresyllione said, "it's a big, crowded city-state. And neither Gedling nor Tuchera's murderers particularly want to be found."

"Well, you need to find Gedling. Our landscaping project is falling *horribly* behind, and I *need* him! I'm a very good friend of Lady Meerka, you know, and if I don't receive satisfaction soon, she will *hear* about it! Let's go, Boslin."

She turned on her heel and departed. Boslin shook his head in confusion and then ran to catch up to her.

Dru rolled his eyes. "Jonas, follow 'em, make sure they don't get lost finding the exit."

Nodding, Jonas also departed quickly, his green cloak billowing behind him.

"Thank you," Rommett said to, basically, the entire squadroom.

"No problem. I just wish we had better news," Dru said.

With a sigh, ban Wyvald said, "Until Gedling turns up or we find our masked conspirators, there's little good news to be had."

"And Quolt still ain't talkin'?" Dru asked.

Tresyllione shook her head.

A confused Rommett asked, "I'm sorry, who's Quolt?"

"One of our masked perpetrators," ban Wyvald said. "Unfortunately, he refuses to give up his three compatriots."

"He goes before the magistrate later today," Tresyllione said.

Rommett nodded. "Good. Perhaps once he's sentenced to death, he'll change his tune." He turned to Dru. "Captain, may I speak to you in private?"

"Sure. C'mon into my office."

As Dru and Rommett went back to the captain's lair, Manfred put a hand out onto Dru's arm. "Hey, Captain—thanks. It meant a lot, you standin' up for me like that."

"Part'a the job," Dru said with a smile. "Don't worry 'bout it."

Rommett went into Dru's office, thinking about the Fansarris and his relationship—such as it was—with them in comparison to Dru's with his detectives. He found the former appallingly lacking, and wondered what that said about his life as an aristocrat…

SIXTEEN

"I'M TELLING YOU, THEY'RE SLEEPING TOGETHER."

Gonzal rolled his eyes at Jayson's declaration as they approached one of the warehouses on the prosaically named Storage Path, where many of the boats that docked at Cliff's End stored their wares that weren't bound for immediate sale. In particular, items from the south that were going to places inland were stored there to eventually be brought to the clearing outside the forest where caravans would take them the rest of the way.

"I refuse to believe that Sergeant Mannit is sleeping with Captain Xerith."

Jayson huffed. "Why not? It's obvious, if you ask me."

"Well, I didn't ask you, so there's that. But if you *did* ask me, I'd tell you that Xerith is only in Cliff's End for a few months a year, she almost never leaves her boat, and also the sarge is, like, a thousand years old. I doubt he can even get it up anymore."

"They got potions for that," Jayson said, "and I've seen the sarge's house. He's got almost no furniture, and all he ever eats is cheap-ass berries and the cruddiest cuts of meat. He don't spend on nothin' else, so I'm willing to bet he buys a potion from Shrenthorshi's place on the River Walk and goes to her boat every time she docks and they do it."

At this point, they were at their destination, which was the warehouse owned and operated by the *Esmerelda*. Several deckhands were carrying boxes into the warehouse, under the supervision of the first mate, a dwarf named Borlanig.

"Keep it goin', lads and lassies, we gotta get movin' before— Oh, hey Jayson, Gonzal, what brings the Castle Guard here today? Out for a stroll?"

"We don't stroll, Borlanig, you know that," Jayson said. "We gotta check your cargo."

Borlanig winced. "And you gotta do it today?"

"Yeah, we do."

"How much to wait till tomorrow?"

"Nice try, but you know that shit don't fly no more," Gonzal said. Back in the old days when Sergeant Gaffni was in charge, graft was the order of the day in Mermaid. Even Jayson and Gonzal—who did not consider themselves to be in the least bit corrupt—would regularly take a copper here and a silver there to look the other way, long as it was something harmless.

But since Sergeant Mannit came out of retirement and took over Mermaid, they'd been keeping a tight lid on things. And while Gonzal couldn't speak for Jayson, he himself had never been comfortable with the bribes. He mostly did it because everyone was.

Now everyone wasn't, and he could sleep at night better.

Having said that, there was a way to deal with this that would, if nothing else, save time.

"Tell you what, Borlanig," Gonzal said. "We're lookin' for somethin' *real* specific. You're unloadin' here, right?"

"Yeah, stuff we got from Saptor Isle. Then we gotta take the stuff *goin'* to Saptor tomorrow mornin'."

"Okay, so whatever you're bringin' in? We don't care about." Gonzal pointed at the open door to the warehouse, through which various deckhands were going.

Jayson said, "What we *do* care about it is some harpy eggs that was stolen from the castle."

Borlanig rubbed his chin and tapped his left foot. "*Harpy* eggs, you say? Hm. Well, we don't really traffic in that sorta thing—Captain Zaile, he stopped carryin' eggs a buncha years back 'cause'a the one time a buncha them hatched on him. Made a *huge* mess."

Gonzal looked at Jayson. Jayson looked at Gonzal. They both sighed. "Which box are the harpy eggs in, Borlanig?"

"What?" Borlanig drew himself up to his not-very-full height. "I just got finished tellin' ya, we don't *do* that no more!"

"Yeah, and you were lyin' through what few teeth you got left," Gonzal said.

Jayson added, "You rubbed your chin and tapped your foot. You always do that when you're lyin'."

Gonzal winced. You should never tell an idiot what his tells are. But he said nothing, as it wouldn't do for the two of them to get into an argument in front of said idiot.

"Look, either give us the harpy eggs or we look through *every* crate."

Borlanig sighed. "That's — I — I mean — it — Oh, hell." His shoulders slumped, and he stared down at the ground. "Dammit. Zaile's gonna kill me."

Jayson smiled. "When he yells at you, just remind him that you kept us away from all the *other* contraband."

"It ain't gonna help." He shook his head and led them inside. "Let's get this shit over with."

They went into the warehouse, where sailors were piling crates on top of each other.

"They're over here." Borlanig pointed at one corner of the building, and started walking that way. Jayson followed him.

Gonzal, though, held back, because one of the sailors looked familiar.

He called out. "Hey, Jayson, you got that crystal we got at roll call?"

"Yeah." Jayson reached into the pouch attached to his belt and pulled it out. "Right here. Why?"

Silently, Gonzal pointed at the familiar-looking sailor, who was helping two others balance a crate on top of another that was exactly the same size.

"Shit." Jayson concentrated, and then the crystal glowed a bright red and the image of a person who looked exactly like the sailor in question appeared floating over the crystal. It was Gedling, the person that Lieutenants Tresyllione and ban Wyvald were after, the one who had been the intended target of those guys in hobgoblin masks who killed a *bahrlan* the other day.

Dammit, Barlin refugee, not bahrlan, Gonzal corrected himself mentally. Everyone around the docks was calling them "*bahrlans*," and he'd been falling into the habit just from exposure. But Sergeant Mannit had also been very clear that guards were *not* to be heard using the term. And honestly Gonzal felt bad just thinking it.

Then he asked Boralnig, "Who's that?"

"Some *bahrlan* we hired yesterday. Wanted t'go one-way to Saptor in exchange for bein' a deckhand for the trip out. Long's he's willin' to work for free, we'll take it."

"It's refugee," Jayson said.

"Excuse me?" Borlanig asked.

Gonzal replied, "Call them refugees, not *bahrlans*."

"S'what everyone calls 'em," Borlanig said with a shrug.

"Whatever, you ain't gettin' him for the journey to Saptor." Gonzal moved toward the sailor in question. "Hey! Gedling!"

Gedling looked up and over at the two guards. Then, upon sighting them and what they were wearing, he turned and ran out of the warehouse.

"Shit!" Gonzal started giving chase. He *hated* it when they ran...

Jayson followed, calling back to Boralnig. "We're gonna be back for those eggs!"

"Yeah, yeah," Gonzal heard Borlanig say, but by then he was outside. He saw Gedling running annoyingly quickly down Storage Path toward the docks.

Gonzal was already out of breath by the time they reached the dock itself. It was a cool autumn day, at least, but running in leather armor always sucked, and he could feel the sweat pouring off his face, even as the breeze from the Garamin Sea evaporated it.

Once they got to the docks, Gonzal looked around and couldn't find Gedling. It was, as usual, a morass of people all over the docks, boarding, disembarking, bartering, loading, unloading, and so on. Every dock was occupied, and Gonzal could see a bunch of ships in the distance that were probably waiting for a berth. *They can't open that extension soon enough*, he thought.

"Where the hell is he?" Jayson asked between deep breaths.

"I don't—" Then he saw their quarry running toward the edge of the boardwalk. "There!"

Just as they started running, however, Gedling leapt *into* the sea.

And then Gonzal couldn't see anything, because a huge crowd of people all converged upon that section of boardwalk, as everyone wanted to see why some shitbrain had decided to dive into the Garamin.

"Excuse us! Coming through! Let us through, please!" Gonzal and Jayson both were pushing their way through the crowds.

By the time they forced their way to the edge of the boardwalk, they could only see a very distant figure swimming away.

"You have *got* to be kidding me," Jayson said.

Gonzal turned to the people next to him. "That's the same one who jumped in, right?"

A gnome said, "Yeah—never seen nobody swim so fast."

With a sigh, Gonzal looked at Jayson. "I can't swim."

"I can—but on my best day, I can't swim that fast, and I couldn't do it in this." He pointed up and down at his armor. "We could try to commandeer a boat?"

Snorting, Gonzal said, "Yeah, good luck with that. By the time we talked one of these dockrats into goin' along with it, Gedling'd be *long* gone. Shit!"

"You know what the worst part of this is?" Jayson asked.

"Worse than losing a guy we were standing twelve handslengths from?" Gonzal asked back.

"Yeah, worse than that—one of us has to tell Lieutenant Tresyllione what happened."

Gonzal's heart started beating even faster than it was from his exertions. "Oh, dammit."

"Hey, maybe we'll be lucky, and it'll be Torin we talk to."

"Based on the way today's goin', we ain't got that kinda luck. C'mon."

Gonzal started pushing his way back through the crowd.

Jayson followed. "C'mon where? We gonna tell the sarge we screwed up?"

"No, we're goin' back to the warehouse first. I ain't havin' that conversation with Mannit 'less we got the harpy eggs in our hands."

Grinning, Jayson said, "Smart move. Let's go."

SEVENTEEN

"How could you let him get away like that?"

Torin smiled with amusement at Danthres, who was directing considerable ire at Jayson and Gonzal. The two Mermaid Precinct guards had just come to the castle to shame-facedly explain that they'd found Gedling, but lost him when he jumped off the boardwalk and swam away.

Danthres continued, "We've had every guard in the city-state looking for this shitbrain, and you had him and you *lost* him!"

Jayson said, "As Wiate is my witness, Lieutenant, I ain't never seen anyone swim that fast."

"For that matter," Gonzal added, "I ain't never seen nobody *run* that fast when he tear-assed it outta the warehouse."

"We didn't even get to talk to him," Jayson said. "Soon's he *saw* we were guards, he was gone. This guy don't wanna talk to you, Lieutenant."

"Well, right now, I don't want to talk to you." Danthres turned to Torin, who was still sitting at his desk while Danthres had been berating the pair of guards. "The prisoners are coming in from Manticore in an hour—Ferdie's supposed to be released. I'm gonna go down to the docks and make sure he remembers what I look like."

"I'm sure," Torin said, "that even after six years, he remembers." Ferdie was a half-dwarf, half-gnome who enjoyed beating up women he picked up in taverns, whom Danthres and Torin had arrested half a dozen years previous. "But have fun. We got the final paperwork courier'd from Velessa on Voran. He was boiled in oil last week. I'm going to go over that and put it in the file."

Danthres nodded. "Enjoy." She looked at Jayson and Gonzal. "I'd better not bump into you two in Mermaid any time soon." Then she turned on her heel and exited the squadroom.

As soon as she was gone, both guards breathed a sigh of relief.

Torin looked up at the two guards and said, "I'm surprised you both came. Usually when someone has to give Danthres bad news, they flip a coin to see who gets the unlucky task."

Gonzal chuckled. "We thought about that. But Sergeant Mannit said it'd be better if we both went. She'd have to split her bein' pissed off between the two of us."

"Probably a wise move."

"Hey," Jayson asked, "isn't Voran that guy who killed the Pirate Queen?"

Torin nodded. "Since it was revealed after she died that the Pirate Queen was the sister of Queen Marta, the king and queen elected to enforce the law stating that anyone with the proved intent to murder a member of the royal family is boiled in oil. Apparently that has finally happened."

Captain Dru came out of his office, then. "Hey, Jayson, Gonzal. It true what I heard, that you found those harpy eggs that Madam Sephina was carryin' on about?"

Jayson nodded, and Gonzal said, "They were bein' smuggled out on the *Esmerelda*."

Dru chuckled. "Zaile's prob'ly spittin' nails. I was just gonna go tell Madam Sephina the good news—wanna come with?"

Gonzal and Jayson exchanged confused glances. "To talk to Madam Sephina?"

"Why not? It's good for those shitbrain aristocrats to see who does the *real* work."

"Um, okay," Jayson said.

Gonzal was grinning. "Let's do it."

The three of them left. Torin was now alone in the squadroom, and he walked over the picture window. He closed his eyes and tried to remember the phrase that Dannee had taught everyone in the detective squad. "*Guvni fan hel heriox* Voran."

The face of Ep formed on the window. "Your accent's getting better," Ep said as the file in question disgorged from his mouth.

"*Seefa*," Torin said with a grin, using the word in Imprata for "thank you."

Their ability to work with Ep had improved tremendously since they started speaking to him in his native language. Where in the past, items would routinely get misfiled, and he would regularly give the wrong file out, now everything had been running much more smoothly. Torin was very grateful to Dannee—who was fluent in Imprata—for teaching them some basic phrases to use.

He brought the file over to his desk and flipped through it, eventually finding the right spot to place the confirmation that Voran's sentence had been carried out.

One slip of parchment fell out, and Torin picked it up off the floor. It was an account of Voran's time in the hole, the dungeon beneath the castle. One of the things listed was his one and only visitor during his time incarcerated, before he was moved to Velessa.

Voran had spent the months prior to his arrival in Cliff's End as the cook on the Pirate Queen's ship, and before that was in Treemark and Iaron. From what he and Danthres had determined, Voran had never set foot in Cliff's End until *Rising Jewel* docked there following Voran's murder of the Pirate Queen.

That visitor was named Willard Macan. Who was he, and why did he visit Voran?

And why was the name so familiar?

Manfred and Kellan walked in, then.

"I can't believe they only got two years," Kellan muttered.

Shaking his bald head, Manfred said, "Hell, the way things've been lately, I was half-expectin' the magistrate to let 'em off. If Tristan had actually *been* from Barlin? I ain't sure Worlin and Paytra would've even been *sent* to Manticore."

It was seeing Manfred, and remembering him complaining about the Fansarris, that made him realize where he'd heard the name Willard Macan recently.

"Manfred," Torin said, looking up at his fellow detective. "The Fansarris have a servant named Willard Macan, don't they?"

"Yeah, I think so." Manfred frowned, then snapped his fingers and his face lit up. "Yeah, he was a pageboy or somethin'. Why?"

"It's odd that their pageboy would be visiting Voran in the hole, isn't it?" Then Torin peered more closely at the date of the visit. "Damnation. Look at the date. It was right after this visit that Voran said he was adamant that he would not give up his cohorts in that Cabal for a Better Flingaria."

Kellan frowned. "I remember that he was adamant the whole time."

"He'd been starting to show signs of cracking. I think the notion of boiling in oil was starting to become a reality and he was reconsidering. Then, one day, he was back to being adamant. We hadn't known at the time that he'd had a visitor. The timing is more than a little suspicious." Torin got up from his desk and grabbed his cloak from the pegboard.

"Where you goin'?" Kellan asked.

"To talk to the Fansarris."

"Better you than me," Manfred muttered.

Torin departed the castle, and headed down into Unicorn Precinct to the mansion on the corner of Meerka and Shade Ways.

He knocked on the door, which was answered by a young boy, who was looking down at the floor as he spoke. "C'n I help you?"

"That depends — are you Willard Macan?"

"Yeah."

"Then you can help me very easily. A few months ago, you came to the castle and visited a prisoner named Voran."

"Yeah."

"Why did you visit him?"

"No reason."

Torin blinked. "You just randomly visited a prisoner in the hole?"

"Yeah."

"For no reason?"

"Yeah."

Boslin Fansarri pushed his way past the pageboy and stood in the doorway. "Lieutenant, why are you bothering our servant?"

"Merely asking him why he was visiting a prisoner in the hole a few months back by the name of Voran."

"We sent him there," Boslin said. "We knew Voran from when we spent a summer in Iaron. We heard about his arrest and were concerned, so we sent Willard to talk to him, see if he needed anything. According to Willard, he said he did not."

"Why did you not go yourself?" Torin asked.

"He killed the Pirate Queen — who, it turns out, was the queen's sister! It wouldn't do for people of my wife's and my station to be seen visting such a person, now would it?"

"I see." In truth, Torin didn't entirely believe what Boslin was telling him — but he had no proof that he was lying, and his story was somewhat reasonable on the face of it. "I would like to question Willard further, if I may, regarding—"

"Out of the question," Boslin said, quickly. "Good day, Lieutenant."

With that, he closed the door in Torin's face.

Torin stared at the closed door and sighed. Were he anywhere but Unicorn Precinct, he would force his way inside with the full authority of the lord and lady, but doing so with aristocrats was a course of action that could be fraught with consequences.

While he weighed the pros and cons of kicking the door down, he saw a little girl running toward him. It was Gerr, one of the youth squad. "Hey, Torin! Danthres tol' me t'find ya! Says they found Gedling!"

"That's good news," Torin said, relieved that something was going right in the investigation.

"Nah, it ain't," Gerr said. "Prison ship found his body floatin' in the Garamin on its way back from Manticore Precinct."

Torin sighed. He flipped Gerr a copper

"Thanks, Torin!" Gerr said after catching the copper, and ran off.

Then Torin left the Fansarri mansion behind for the time being, instead heading in a southwesterly direction down Meerka Way toward the docks.

Hope you're happy, Quolt. It seems you got your desire to see that particular refugee dead after all...

EIGHTEEN

CRELLIN QUOLT SAT IMPATIENTLY WAITING FOR THE MAGISTRATE TO RETURN.

He had sat through the entire procedure from the small table in the magistrate's chambers, a high-ceilinged room in the north wing of the castle that included the table at which Quolt was sitting, the much larger desk at which the magistrate would sit, a small gallery for spectators and witnesses (currently empty), plus another chair for the magistrate's clerk.

At the moment, Quolt was sitting alone with two Swords assigned to Gryphon Precinct. The clerk came in at some point, and started making notes, but still no sign of the magistrate.

While sitting in his chair at the small table, Quolt had watched the dwarf Sword they'd bribed, Ungrilig, testify that Quolt had paid him to look the other way when they attacked various bahrlans, and that he got more to do so when they were going after Gedling. He observed the two Cloaks testify that Tuchera was the victim, not Gedling. And the clerk presented the red hobgoblin mask that the Castle Guard had found in his room. Then the magistrate had left the room to deliberate, which had struck Quolt as a waste of time. But maybe the old man had to relieve himself or something.

Finally, the magistrate reentered, limping toward his desk. His snow-white short curly hair was a direct contrast to his mahogany skin.

Very slowly, he sat down in his chair — which was much more comfortable than Quolt's, which he supposed was to be expected — and let out a difficult breath. Quolt wondered how long he'd been serving as Cliff's End's magistrate; from the looks of him, it had to have gone back to roughly the time of the dragonriders a thousand years earlier...

He wished they would get this over with, so he could get back to his life. Why even go through this charade?

"We've heard all the testimony and the evidence," the magistrate said in a deep voice. "Before we pass sentence on your pathetic self, it behooves me to ask if you have anything to say for yourself."

Quolt recoiled from the contempt in the magistrate's voice. "I, uh—" He swallowed. "I don't—I don't understand."

"I'm about to condemn you, young man, so this is your chance to say something in your defense in the likely vain hope that you'll live to see midwinter."

His eyes went wide. "Live? What do you mean?"

The magistrate peered across at Quolt with a vicious, penetrating gaze. "You do understand that you *killed* a man?"

"I killed a *bahrlan*, sure. It's not like I killed a citizen of *this* city-state."

Turning to his clerk, the magistrate said, "Jode, is there an address of record for the victim, Tuchera?"

"Yes, sir."

"Is that address located within the borders of the demesne of Cliff's End?"

"Yes, sir."

Now again fixing his pitiless gaze upon Quolt, the magistrate said, "It would seem Tuchera *is* a citizen of this city-state."

"Well, yeah," Quolt said, "but he wasn't even who we were supposed to hit! It was a mistake!"

"Oh, it absolutely was," the magistrate said angrily. "And one you will pay for with your life, absent your testimony providing some mitigating circumstance."

Quolt swallowed.

He also remembered the words that ugly half-elf lieutenant had said when they arrested him: *"The only way you're going to avoid being hanged is if you give up your three cohorts."*

"So," the magistrate said, "if you *don't* have anything to say—"

"No, no, I do." Quolt got to his feet. "I didn't do this alone, and if I'm dying, I ain't dying alone."

"We already know you didn't act alone," the magistrate said. "Are you now willing to provide us with the names of your co-conspirators?"

"Damn right, I am."

"Very well. Sentence will be postponed pending the outcome of this revelation. You will remain in custody here in the castle dungeon until such a time as we can determine that your information was of use to the cause of the lord and lady's justice, and we will reconsider sentencing then." He looked over at one of the two Swords. "Abrik, get him out of my sight and back to Lieutenants Tresyllione and ban Wyvald."

"You betcha, sir," the Sword said. He grabbed Quolt by the shoulders and yanked him to his feet with unnecessary force.

"Hey! Take it easy!"

Once he was on his feet, Quolt shrugged off the guard's grip, but did allow himself to be guided toward the exit and into a corridor.

They worked their way through a bunch of corridors that were all filled with ass-ugly tapestries until they came back to the room where the Cloaks worked.

A Cloak holding a bunch of parchments met them as they entered.

"'Ey, Sarge, this shitbrain's, like, gotta talk to Torin an' Danthres. Said he wants to, like, give up his shitbrain friends."

"I thought you weren't giving up your shitbrain friends," the sergeant said with a nasty smile.

"I ain't dyin' for those guys," Quolt muttered.

To Abrik, the sergeant said, "Put him in two."

"C'mon." Abrik pushed Quolt toward one of the doors on the south side of the squadroom.

Once again, Quolt found himself sitting alone in a room. It was a state of affairs he was really getting sick of, whether it was one of these interrogation rooms, the cell in the hole, or the magistrate's chambers.

Then the two Cloaks entered. Without preamble, the ugly half-elf bitch said, "I have some good news for you, Quolt. You finally got your victim!"

Quolt frowned. "Huh?"

"Gedling. His body turned up in the Garamin Sea. So your mission has been accomplished after all."

"Great."

"Fascinating," the redheaded Cloak said as he sat in the chair opposite Quolt. "I would have imagined you to be thrilled that the 'filthy *bahrlan*' you were after finally received his comeuppance, or some such absurdity."

"Right now, I could give a shit about *bahrlans*. I just don't wanna be hanged, okay? Magistrate said if I name the other three, he won't hang my ass."

"Oh, we'll need more than that, I'm afraid," the half-elf said. "You see, you're currently an unemployed dockworker. You don't have the funds to bribe Ungrilig. So unless one of your three co-conspirators is very wealthy, we'll also need the name of your patron."

"Fine, whatever, long as I don't get hanged, right?"

The redhead nodded. "That is the arrangement, yes."

"Fine. Guy what paid us is named Sozin."

The two Cloaks exchanged glances. "Jerri Donoh's toady," the half-elf said.

"Why would a criminal pay you to assault Barlin refugees?" the redhead asked Quolt.

"The hell should I know? The hell should I care, neither, they paid us. We needed the money—like you said, we're unemployed."

"All four of you?" the half-elf prompted.

Quolt nodded. "Me, Creffath, Embo Markov, and Jak Reesh."

The redhead nearly fell out of his chair. "Say that final name again, please."

Swallowing nerviously, Quolt said, "J-Jak Reesh. He's a—he's a carpenter. Why, you know him?"

"I do."

Up until that point, the person in the room Quolt was the most scared of was the half-elf. She was ugly, she was mean, she was intimidating, and every time he looked at her, he expected her to disembowel him.

The redhead, meanwhile, had been pleasant and friendly, even when snottily referring to filthy *bahrlans* in order to try to make fun of Quolt. But when he said, "I do," his voice dropped an octave or two, and Quolt actively feared for his life in a way that even the half-elf couldn't manage.

Getting to his feet, the redhead said, "Excuse me," and left the interrogation room.

"What's—" Quolt started. "What's with him?"

The half-elf stared at the door for a second, then turned back to Quolt, leaning forward and resting her clenched fists on the table as she got into his face. Quolt could smell the tea on her breath, and he once again was getting that about-to-get-disemboweled feel.

"You're sure Jak Reesh is one of your hobgoblin-mask-wearing gaggle?"

"Absolutely. He *hates* the *bahrlans* more'n any of us. Bastards took all the carpentry work."

For several seconds, the half-elf just stared at him.

Then she left the room without a word.

Dunno what you did to piss off the Cloaks, Jak, but for your sake, you'd better not be home when they call…

NINETEEN

JAK REESH PUT THE KEY INTO THE LOCK OF THE DOOR OF HIS PRIVATE ROOM, the yelling of his landlay echoing in his ears, still.

He'd had to move down to a single room after losing his previous apartment, which he'd moved to after losing his house. Well, okay, he didn't lose the house, Ella threw him out because she got tired of him not paying his half of the expenses like he promised he would when he moved in.

Who knew that it would be so hard to maintain work as a carpenter in Cliff's End?

And now he was a week from being kicked out of this place.

Maybe I can talk Torin into letting me move in with him.

The lock didn't tumble open when the turned the key, which concerned him. Apparently, he left it unlocked? Pulling down the handle, the door opened.

Then he walked in to see Torin ban Wyvald sitting in his easy chair.

"Torin! This is a nice surprise! I was just about to—"

"Be quiet, please, Jak," Torin said in a very quiet tone—indeed, quieter than Jak had ever heard Torin speak when he wasn't whispering or trying to be discreet.

"What's—what's wrong, Torin?"

"Several months ago, Danthres offered to look into your employment history on my behalf. I was concerned, you see, because you'd lost so many jobs in succession. I was concerned that there might have been some manner of issue—one that you may not even have been aware of."

Jak drew himself up straight. "You had Danthres *investigate* me?"

"She volunteered, and I wanted to be sure that everything was all right with you. It didn't take her long to discover the two common threads in your job history, however. One was your consistent absences from work. The other was that they were all non-guild positions."

"I can't afford the dues the guild wants—"

"And the people who hire non-guild carpenters know that, so they can pay you less. Which is why even the jobs you have had have been low-paying—but then you kept getting terminated for frequent absences, which is the sort of thing that gets around."

Jak did not like the way this conversation was going. "Look—"

"Do you know what you've been telling me for the last several months? That you can't get work because of the Barlin refugees. Well, in fact, you've been calling them *bahrlans*, even though I've asked you *repeatedly* not to use that term. But the only reason you're in competition with refugees is because you're going after non-guild jobs—the refugees also can't afford guild dues, so they're gravitating to those jobs. And the reason why you're losing out to those refugees is because they actually *turn up* for work."

Closing his eyes and sighing, Jak said, "Look, I know, it's been a problem, but—"

"Also, you've been lying to me about your current employment, as it's *not* a carpentry job." Torin then reached down onto the floor and picked up a yellow hobgoblin mask.

Wincing, Jak said, "I don't suppose I could convince you that I've never seen that before."

"No."

"Look, they paid us to beat up *bahrlans*. And so what? They come in here, they take our jobs, and we're supposed to just *accept* it?"

"Your poor job history predates the Barlin fire, I'm afraid, Jak." Torin got up from the easy chair. "And now two men are dead."

"I'm sorry?"

"Tuchera, whom you killed by mistake, and now Gedling is also dead—he drowned in the Garamin after running away from some guards."

Looking away from Torin's pitiless gaze, Jak said, "I'm sorry. I guess it got a little out of hand, but my boss said we just had to beat him up a little more. I didn't know he was going to die!"

"That's not what Quolt told us."

That caught Jak completely off guard. *He knows Crellin's name!* "Um…"

Holding up a hand, Torin said, "Stop. Stop lying to me. You didn't have carpentry work, you had a job as a *thug* working for a criminal. You were being employed by Jerri Donoh—someone Danthres and I have been clashing with on and off for a decade—to commit criminal acts, one of which resulted in a murder, and which indirectly led to another death."

"I'm sorry, I couldn't—" Jak tried to collect his thoughts. He hadn't been prepared for this. "Crellin told us we had to keep the job secret. *That's* why I didn't tell you."

Torin grabbed him by the shoulders, forcing him to look right at his face, which was uncharacteristically contorted into a rictus of anger. "No, you didn't tell me because I'm a lieutenant in the Castle Guard, and if you told me what you were doing, I would be forced to arrest you. As I'm about to do now."

Jak felt his stomach drop. "You—you can't!"

"Can't I?"

"I mean—we're in a relationship! Is that even allowed?"

"Oh, we're *not* in a relationship any longer, Jak, of that you may be certain."

Closing his eyes, Jak said, "That's not what I meant, I mean—" Then he opened his eyes. "Wait, we're not?"

"I'm afraid I never was able to scrape together the desire to share my bed with a murderer, no. I'm arresting you, Jak Reesh, for assault on multiple citizens of Cliff's End, for the murder of Tuchera, and for conspiracy to commit the murder of Gedling."

Jak pulled himself away from Torin's grip. "So that's it? You just dump me and arrest me?"

"Yes," Torin said with depressing finality.

"I don't get *any* consideration for what we mean to each other?"

"Oh, you have. That consideration is that I came to you alone, in the hopes that you might show some remorse—for the act, perhaps, or for how you betrayed me. It is to my great regret and shame that you've shown none of that. A pity, as I came alone to spare you the spectacle of being arrested by several members of the Castle Guard who would no doubt treat you very physically roughly. As you might imagine, Creffath and Embo Markov are being so arrested even as we speak. And given your response to this consideration—which, as ever, is to take no responsibility for anything bad you've done or failures you've had—I'm sorry I bothered. Come on."

Torin reached out and grabbed Jak by the shoulder.

Jak tried to shrug off the grip. "Get *off* of me!"

Then he punched Torin in the face and turned and ran out his front door.

As he pumped his legs as fast as he could to get away from his erstwhile lover, Jak felt his knuckles start to sting.

He tried to figure out where he might go. Torin had just said that Embo and Creffath were in custody, and Crellin was still in the hole. *Maybe Ella will take me back in?*

Then, just as he was about to turn onto Meerka Way in the hopes of getting lost in the crowds, he was tackled from behind, his face hitting the ground with a bone-jarring impact.

A hand shoved his face into the ground, while knees pressed into his back. His entire body now felt like one big bruise.

And Torin's voice sounded over his head. "As I said, you're under arrest. We can now add resisting arrest to the list of charges."

His face still in the dirt, Jak was unable to say anything.

But he couldn't believe that Torin had betrayed him like this.

I loved him, and he does this *to me?*

As Torin yanked him to his feet and led him down the street—not even doing him the courtesy of allowing him to wipe the dirt off his face—he swore he would get his revenge on Torin for this.

TWENTY

S<small>OZIN STOOD ON LINE AT THE DOCKS FOR THE DINGHY THAT WAS GOING TO</small> take him out to Manticore Precinct.

The Cloaks had tried their usual tricks. Promises of a lighter sentence, promises of an easier time with the magistrate, and other nonsense.

But Sozin knew what side of the scroll the writing was on. Jerri Donoh was the boss, and he did what Jerri said. If he did what he was told and kept his mouth shut, he'd be treated well while imprisoned, and likely promoted when he got out. Jerri's influence on the barge wasn't as strong as it was before it was absorbed by the Castle Guard and made into Manticore Precinct, but it was still enough so that Sozin knew he'd be okay.

It wasn't the first time he'd been incarcerated doing work for Jerri.

There was that time he got caught with the bootleg glamours that Jerri was shopping around. Sozin just happened to be in the warehouse when the Swords and Cloaks came into bust the shipment. Sozin claimed that they were his—even though he truly was in the warehouse for other reasons.

There was the time when someone had to take the fall for beating up Horvat, because Yarvik—who actually *did* beat up Horvat—was needed for another job in Treemark. Yarvik got on the caravan to Treemark and Sozin spent six months on the barge.

And then there was the time five years ago when Jerri had master-minded a theft that they'd covered up with a Scaff charm. That turned out to be a massive tactical error. Yes, the Scaff charm covered up who committed the theft on the peel-back the Cloaks' pet wizard did, but it also left behind a distinctive signature that made it even easier to track them down.

Sozin knew the deal. In fact, one of the guards who was in charge of the dinghy was his old pal Brokk. When he got to the front of the line, Brokk, along with another guard he didn't know, was checking names on a slate.

Without even looking up from the slate, Brokk intoned dully, "Name?"

"Brokk, it's me."

Now he did look up. "Sozin? Mitre's bones, what are you doing back here?"

"Paid someone to do something bad."

"Well, getcher ass on the boat, we got a schedule t'meet."

Nodding, Sozin stepped on the boat.

Brokk grabbed his arm as he did so. "And come see me at chowtime, I'll show you the right table."

"Thanks, Brokk."

As he searched for a seat on the dinghy, Sozin heard the other guard ask, "Why you talkin' to that shitbrain like he's your friend?"

"He's Jerri Donoh's right hand."

"Yeah, so?"

Sozin sighed. That had to have been a new recruit.

He looked for a seat, now out of earshot of Brokk and his partner, nodding to the people he knew on board. There was Falbrat, probably back in for pickpocketing tourists on the River Walk. Next to him was Emma Lancas, who was a talented grifter with poor taste in lovers — if she was on her way back to the barge, it meant she'd taken on some idiot as a partner again, and that partner got her arrested. And behind her was Trethen lothHratha, who had a seat open next to her.

"Sozin," she said as he took that open seat.

"What're you doing here, Trethen?"

"Trafficking in stolen goods."

Wincing, Sozin said, "You mean those saddles you were selling were stolen?"

"Oh, no, don't be ridiculous. Why would I sell stolen saddles? No, those magickal saddlebags were stolen from some wizard or other."

Now, Sozin's eyes widened. "You stole from a *wizard*?"

"Oh, no, don't be ridiculous," she said again. "My dealer stole from a wizard."

"And the brotherhood didn't turn you into a newt?"

"Me? No. My dealer? Possibly. I gave him up, which is why I'm just getting a couple months on the barge."

"You gave up your dealer?"

"When the brotherhood's breathing down my neck? Absolutely. I can find another dealer, I can't find another life."

Sozin had to concede that point. You didn't mess with the magick-users any more than you had to, and Trethen was far better off sticking with the magistrate than whatever the brotherhood might have had in store for the person who stole from them.

Once everyone was on board, the dinghy was untethered from the dock and started moving out into the Garamin.

Brokk stood at the front of the dinghy while the boat was being rowed by four guards, two at the fore, two aft.

"For those of you who've never been incarcerated on the barge before, you will be outfitted with bracelets upon arrival at Manticore Precinct. As long as you remain on the barge in designated areas, the bracelets will simply be bracelets. However, should you try to leave the barge, or go to a restricted area like the bridge or the engine room or the guard lounge, the runes on the bracelets will activate and make the bracelets incredibly heavy. Do yourself a favor, don't go where you're not supposed to go."

Brokk went on, talking about when mealtimes were, what facilities were available. To Sozin's surprise, there was now a gymnasium.

Once Brokk was finished, he moved down the dinghy to take a seat. Sozin got his attention as he moved past. "When did they put a gym in?"

Shrugging, Brokk said, "Lord Doval wanted it after they made the barge into Manticore Precinct. Thought maybe people would be less likely to jump overboard if they had more distractions."

"Is it working?"

Again, Brokk shrugged. "There's always idiots jumping overboard."

"Yeah." Sozin nodded to Brokk, who continued to his seat. "I have to admit, I've met a lot of stupid people in my line of work—my employer sometimes makes loans, you see, and most of those are among the greatest fools in all of Cliff's End—but I can't imagine any of them being so idiotic as to jump overboard on the barge when they know it's certain death."

"Never underestimate people's stupidity," Trethen said. "My sister is one of them."

"Your sister?"

Trethen nodded. "She got popped for fraud—selling armor and shields that she claimed were magickally enhanced. The reason why she did it is because the brotherhood charged so much for the type of magick enhancement she was pretending to sell. She figured there was no way the prison would be able to afford to magick that many bracelets, so she figured it was all a lie. And she was a champion swimmer, so she jumped overboard." She sighed. "I was her sole beneficiary, and she left me with a mountain of debt."

"Ouch. I'm sorry," he said.

Eventually, they arrived at the barge, which was now decorated with a giant version of the manticore medallion that also adorned the armor of Brokk and his coworkers.

The prisoners all filed off the dinghy, each being fitted with a pair of metal bracelets as they set foot on the deck. Sozin was informed by the guard who put on his bracelets that he was to report to Group 4.

He joined Group 4, eventually taken to his cell on B Deck.

Later, after the evening meal—Brokk had, as promised, directed him to the best table to sit at, which included several members of Cliff's End's underworld with whom Sozin was acquainted—he stood out on the deck, looking out over the moonlit night. The Garamin was calm this evening, and it looked like the barge was floating on a large piece of obsidian glass.

After a bit, Trethen joined him at the railing.

"It's beautiful, isn't it?" she said.

"It is. Almost doesn't feel like a prison." He held up his arms. "Except for these."

"Yeah. So, remember how I said that my sister left me with her debts when she jumped over this railing and tried to swim away?"

Sozin nodded.

"Those debts are—well, crippling. But I've been given an opportunity to have them paid off."

"That's good."

"For me, yes."

Frowning, Sozin said, "I don't understand, why—"

Trethen then pushed him, hard, into the railing. Sozin struggled to breathe, as the impact with the metal railing at least bruised, and possibly cracked, one of his ribs.

Trethen bent over and grabbed Sozin's legs, tipping him upward so that his head and chest went over the railing.

And then he found himself falling toward the sea.

He crashed head-first into the water, pain wracking his chest and head and neck, from both being shoved into the railing and from the impact with the Garamin's surface.

Sozin tried and failed to lift his arms to try to swim, but now the bracelets felt as if they weighed a ton.

He plummeted toward the seabed, water filling his mouth and nose.

His final thoughts were wondering why Trethen had been hired to kill him. Did Jerri not trust him?

Sozin died not knowing.

TWENTY-ONE

DANTHRES APPROACHED LADY MEERKA'S OFFICE WITH A CERTAIN SENSE OF trepidation, not that she had any objection to meeting with her lady-ship. Meerka had taken a liking to Danthres last year, and Danthres had worked hard to cultivate it. Generally, Danthres viewed playing the politics of the western wing of the castle as beneath her contempt. But she actually *liked* Lady Meerka, and she was one of the two most influential people in the city-state.

But because of that, she knew that altering plans wasn't something her ladyship was particularly fond of, and Danthres hadn't warned her that she was bringing two of her fellow detectives along.

It didn't help that one of those two was practically bouncing.

"I can't believe we're just going to *talk* to Lady Meerka!" Dannee was geebling.

"Do yourself a favor," Danthres said to the half-dwarf, "and do *not* fawn over her. I know most of the aristocrats love that sort of thing, but not Lady Meerka. Speak to her the same way you would speak to anyone you respect. It's what she prefers."

Meerka's secretary got up without a word upon their approach and stuck her head into the office. "Milady, Lieutenants Tresyllione, Ocly, and lothLathna are here."

There was an awkward pause, which was exactly what Danthres had been afraid of.

"I was under the impression that Lieutenant Tresyllione had made the appointment."

"I'm sorry, milady, but all three—"

Danthres stepped forward and put herself in the doorway next to the poor, beleaguered secretary. "I apologize, m'lady, but one of the subjects I wanted to discuss with you would be much easier for Aleta and Dannee to explain than it would be for me."

"Very well, if you say so." Lady Meerka was sitting at her desk, surrounded by slates. She set one aside, picked up another, stared at it, then put it aside as well and looked up at Danthres. "Do come in."

She only had two guest chairs, but Aleta stood at parade rest between the two chairs, leaving Danthres and Dannee to take the two seats.

Meerka was a short, stout woman with curly blond hair, though she had cut her hair so short that the curls were barely noticeable now. She looked up now at Aleta and said, "You're the former Shranlaseth."

"Yes, m'lady. Aleta lothLathna."

"You're the only former Shranlaseth in the Castle Guard. Why is that?"

Aleta shifted her weight from foot to foot.

Danthres hid a smile. Anything that made her elven coworker uncomfortable gave Danthres a certain joy.

"I honestly don't know, m'lady. It seems to me that working for the Castle Guard is the best way to channel our training into something that works for the good of the commonweal."

"That isn't what I meant by my question," Meerka said testily. "Most former Shranlaseth have become assassins — or have taken jobs that have absolutely nothing to do with their former lives. Why did you not follow that trend?"

"As I said, m'lady," Aleta said slowly, "I thought this the best use of my skills. I haven't been put in a position where I've had to kill anyone since I joined the Castle Guard, but I still can make use of my other training, and do some good for the world."

"You believe that the Castle Guard is a force for good, then?"

"Perhaps not always good, m'lady, but for order at the very least. It is a very chaotic world. Being in the Shranlaseth was appealing to me at first because it also was a force for order — but it was order with a terrible price. I prefer the Castle Guard's method of maintaining order to the Elf Queen's."

"Fascinating." Meerka nodded.

Silently, Danthres agreed with her ladyship's assessment. Between that and the revelation the other day about Aleta's early life, she was starting to think she needed to have a significant conversation with the

Shranlaseth, one that wasn't their usual one punctuated by insults and such.

Meerka then looked at Dannee. "You're the daughter of Esta Ocly, are you not?"

Dannee practically beamed, and she sat up even straighter in the chair. "Yes, milady, I am!"

"I saw her perform *Shansheria* in Barlin with my children a decade ago. She was quite good. Does she still perform?"

"Yes, milady, she does — she's part of a theatrical company in Iaron."

"Ah, so she wasn't a victim of the fire, then?"

Dannee shook her head. "No, Father joined an architectural firm in Iaron three years ago, and they moved there from Barlin. I'd already moved to Cliff's End by then."

"Very good." Meerka folded her hands on her desk. "All right, Lieutenant, the other two may join this meeting. What is it you wish to discuss?"

"Two things, actually," Danthres said. "The first is to respectfully request that you approve Captain Dru's request to hire two more detectives for the squad."

That prompted Meerka to shuffle through the slates on her desk, but it wasn't a slate she was after, but rather one of the parchments that was under a pile of slates. "Yes, I have it here. I had not had a chance to properly consider it. You believe it is necessary."

"Extremely so, m'lady," Danthres said emphatically. "We've had a *huge* influx of people, and that has increased the crime rate — but we still have the same number of detectives working those crimes." With a glance back at Aleta, she added, "It's giving chaos much too much of a leg up on order."

"I see." Meerka stared at the parchment for a few seconds, then looked at Aleta. "Do you agree, Lieutenant lothLathna?"

"I do, m'lady. We're struggling to keep up with our cases, and two more detectives will ameliorate that burden." She glanced at Danthres. "As Lieutenant Tresyllione said, it will aid in our maintaining order."

"And you agree?" she asked Dannee.

"Oh, I wouldn't presume to speak for what's best for the detective squad," Dannee said demurely. "I've only been a lieutenant for a few months."

Testily, Meerka said, "Your modesty is unnecessary. I assume you have good observational capabilities, else you would never have been promoted to detective in the first place."

Danthres managed to control her reaction to that. She'd known far too many detectives during her dozen years on the job who had terrible observational capabilities…

Slumping in her chair, Dannee said, "I'm so sorry, I didn't mean to offend you!"

"Your apology is equally unnecessary. Simply answer the question—do you agree that it is best to hire two more detectives?"

"I think it is, yes, milady," Dannee said very quietly.

"Do you truly believe that for a reason, or are you simply telling me what I wish to hear?"

Dannee cleared her throat. "I believe we will be a more efficient unit if we have two more detectives, yes."

"Good. I prefer efficiency, as Lieutenant Tresyllione is aware. And the budget can *easily* accommodate the addition of two more lieutenant salaries."

"It can?" The words came out of Danthres's mouth before she could stop herself.

"Of course it can. I just said it could."

"My apologies, m'lady, but—well, I'm used to hearing cries of budget poverty from this wing of the castle."

"Oh, and often with good reason, but our economy is stronger than ever. The influx of refugees has proven to be an overall boon to the city-state's financial outlook, since they all need to feed, clothe, and house themselves, and there are plenty of jobs. Tourism has also increased tenfold, and that figure will rise once the port extension is complete. In particular, the Lord Kioa Museum has seen its attendance triple since they opened up those memorial exhibits to Gan Brightblade and Olthar lothSirhans, and I've been informed that they're doing a similar exhibit for the Pirate Queen starting next month."

Danthres smiled. The Lord Kioa Museum had been owned and operated by the eponymous lord for decades, but when he died, he left the museum to the demesne itself, so all the museum's profits went right into the government coffers.

"Therefore, given your compelling arguments for it, and given that I have no good financial argument against it, I will approve this requisition."

"Thank you, m'lady," Danthres said, putting a great deal of gratitude into those three words.

"Yes, thank you *so* much!" Dannee said with a big smile.

Aleta just inclined her head.

Meerka folded her hands together on her desk. "Now what is the second matter?"

"A bit more delicate, I'm afraid." Danthres looked up at Aleta.

The ex-Shranlaseth nodded and moved a bit forward. "Dannee and I were ordered to shut down a company called Ankh Security. They have been providing fee-based protection for merchants down Jorbin's Way."

"Who gave that order?"

"Your son, m'lady, but that order was given based on Dannee's and my report that they were charging for protection as a means of extortion. However, further investigation revealed that Ankh Security is a legitimate business that is attempting to supplement the Castle Guard's protection, functioning as an area-specific mutual aid association with security and also an emergency to aid merchants in need."

"I see. What is it you want from me, then?"

Aleta hesitated.

Danthres decided to step in. Aleta was generally respectful to people above her in station, and this didn't call for diplomacy. "Your son still wants Ankh Security to be shut down. We think that it can be useful."

"How so?"

Now Danthres looked at Dannee expectantly. The half-dwarf looked apprehensive, but this *had* been her idea…

She took a breath, and then Dannee started: "A lot of the merchants down Jorbin's Way don't trust the Castle Guard. There are a lot of crimes that go unreported. I think that the fact that Ankh Security isn't directly affiliated with the city-state means that some of the merchants are more willing to go to them for help. Even with the recruiting drive and opening Phoenix Precinct and getting two new detectives—that chaos that Aleta was talking about is just getting worse. I think if we let Ankh reopen for business, it'll be a net good."

"What are the qualifications of these people in Ankh Security?" Meerka asked.

Aleta took this one. "It's run by Rob Wirrn. He was a twenty-two-year veteran in the Castle Guard, and your older son offered him early retirement as part of his campaign to get rid of as many veterans as possible last year."

"Yes, I recall," Meerka said sourly. "Blayk was an idiot in so *many* ways. I'm sorry he had to die in such a horrid way, but I'm not sorry that he's no longer the lord of this demesne."

Danthres thought her ladyship didn't sound all *that* sorry that her oldest son had been boiled in oil, but she wasn't about to say anything about that, not if she valued her continued good relationship with Meerka. Instead, she said, "Most of Ankh's employees are ex-Guard — either retired or left for medical reasons — or ex-military. Or both."

"And do you not think that their function is redundant, given that protection of the people of the demesne is the job of the Castle Guard?"

Dannee looked away briefly, and then shyly said, "That was also my initial objection, milady. But — for the moment, at least — we're stretched thin. It's possible that the supplement they provide will only be needed for a limited time. But that doesn't change the fact that it's needed."

"Besides which," Aleta said, "the account they've created with the Cliff's End Bank is one that will be very useful to any merchants who fall prey to crimes."

"You've verified this account?" Meerka asked.

Dannee nodded. "We spoke to Amilar Grovis directly, and he showed us the affidavit that both he and Wirrn signed that the monies in the account will only be used for charitable purposes."

"Interesting." Meerka stared ahead at some indeterminate point on the wall behind Danthres. This, Danthres knew, meant she was thinking, and often made for awkward silences.

Luckily, this one only lasted about seven seconds.

"I will need more information before I reverse one of my son's decisions. That is not a thing I may do cavalierly if the city-state is to continue to run smoothly. I will speak with this Rob Wirrn, and also with the Grovis family. Is there anything else?"

"No, m'lady," Danthres said as she got to her feet. Dannee followed suit a second later.

"Very well. Good day to you all." Meerka then went back to studying slates.

They left the office and headed back toward the eastern wing. "That was amazing!" Dannee said.

"That was not what I expected," Aleta said. "She is — much different than I imagined."

Danthres chuckled. "That's what most people think."

As soon as they entered the squadroom, she saw Torin removing his cloak from the pegboard. "Ah, Danthres, good. Come, we need to hie ourselves to Clara's Place."

Frowning, Danthres asked, "What for?"

"We got a report from Manticore that Sozin was killed on the barge."

That surprised Danthres even more than the notion that they were going to Clara's Place, though given that Sozin's boss hung out at that restaurant, it made more sense now.

Dannee said, "We'll tell Captain Dru how the meeting went."

Nodding to Dannee, Danthres then regarded her partner. "What happened?"

"The suspect in that murder is being sent over on the dinghy, so we'll find out when they get here, but a messenger just arrived saying that Jerri Donoh wishes to give us a statement."

Now Danthres was completely confused. "His chief flunky was just killed, and he *wants* to talk to *us?*"

"Indeed."

"Jerri *never* wants to talk to us."

"No, he doesn't. Curious, no?"

"Very. Let's go." Danthres followed Torin out of the squadroom.

TWENTY-TWO

BOSLIN FANSARRI SAT IN THE INTERVIEW ROOM IN THE EASTERN WING OF THE castle with a strange combination of impatience and gratitude.

The former was because he had been sitting here for half an hour. A guard had come to their house and said that they had vital information about the conspiracy that had targeted their landscapers. Boslin had said to the guard that he thought they were targeted because they were *bahrlans*, but the guard said he didn't know anything about that, he was just under orders to bring Boslin to the castle.

The latter was because it was *quiet*. Life with Elmira rarely led to moments of silence, and he found it very refreshing.

Then the two lieutenants, ban Wyvald and Tresyllione, came in.

"We're so sorry to keep you watiting," ban Wyvald said, "but we have some information that may be of interest to you."

"Yes, the guard who brought me here said as much, but—" Boslin hesitated. "I'm sorry, but Gedling is dead, yes?"

"He is, yes," ban Wyvald said.

Tresyllione added, "But it's how he died that's of interest. You see, he drowned."

"Why is that of interest?" Boslin asked, confused.

"He was an excellent swimmer," ban Wyvald said. "According to the witnesses, including the two guards he ran away from, he was, in fact, a superlative swimmer. It's odd that he would then turn up drowned."

"It happens, I suppose. What I don't understand is why you think that matters to me. He was a *bahrlan*. They've been getting attacked a lot, haven't they?"

"But that's the odd thing," Tresyllione said. "Most of the refugees who've been assaulted have been randomly attacked. But Gedling was specifically targeted."

"Worse," ban Wyvald added, "he was the original target, but they killed Tuchera instead. But this wasn't simply a matter of someone beating up a random refugee. The people who paid the killers specifically told them to target the landscaper working for the Fansarris."

"I see." This was starting to make Boslin nervous.

"What we're worried about," Tresyllione said, "is that your family might have been targeted. We wanted to talk to you some more about your friendship with Voran."

At this point, Boslin was completely confused about what the two lieutenants were talking about. "What does some *bahrlan* working for us getting killed have to do with Voran?"

"Possibly quite a bit," ban Wyvald said. "You see, Voran was part of a conspiracy known as the Cabal for a Better Flingaria."

"We don't know *that* much about this cabal," Tresyllione said, and she sounded very reluctant to admit that. "In fact, we only know the name because Voran told it to us in this very room. But it seems that this cabal is less than happy with the leadership of King Marcus and Queen Marta, given that they conspired to have them replaced by the Pirate Queen."

"But that makes this cabal very much a target," ban Wyhvald said. "After all, the king and queen are quite popular. It's possible that someone might be targeting associates. And you yourself told us that Voran was a friend of yours."

"Well, yes, but—" Boslin squirmed in his seat.

"So," ban Wyvald continued, not giving Boslin a chance to formulate a coherent response, "we're going to have to station a guard from Unicorn Precinct at your house."

Boslin's eyes widened. "Excuse me?"

"And," Tresyllione added, "the M.E. will have to cast a peel-back at your house."

"Wait, *what*?" Now Boslin was filled with revulsion. While he didn't share his wife's dislike for magick, Boslin had never liked wizards, and didn't want any of them near his home. "Absolutely not!"

"It's a simple—" ban Wyvald started.

"No!" Boslin got to his feet. "I will not have wizards tramping through my house!"

Ban Wyvald tried again. "It's standard procedure when a crime's been committed."

"Please sit down, Mr. Fansarri," Tresyllione said in a low, menacing tone.

"Or what? I've had it with this treatment! First you come at me with wild theories about strange conspiracies, and then you threaten to send *wizards* to *my* house! I will not stand for this! Gedling was just some landscaper who overheard something he shouldn't have, and then—"

Boslin cut himself off quickly, realizing he said more than he should, but Tresyllione pounced on it.

"What did he overhear?"

"Nothing." Boslin sat back down. "Just some personal things, Things that were none of his business, truly. We were honestly thinking of firing him for listening in on our personal conversations, but then he got sick and disappeared, so it wound up not mattering, especially once he died."

"So," ban Wyvald said, "he didn't, perhaps, overhear your plans as members of the Cabal for a Better Flingaria?"

"What?" Boslin tried very hard to sound convincingly confused here. "Don't be absurd! Elmira and I are *completely* loyal to the king and queen! Always have been! The only organization that Elmira and I are a part of is Flingarians Against Wizards. And believe you me, when next we have one of our meetings, the appalling behavior of the Castle Guard will be at the *top* of the agenda! Sending wizards to people's *houses*, it's just—"

Leaning back in her chair, Tresyllione said, "I'm glad you brought FAW up, as we noticed a name on your membership rolls."

Boslin's face fell. "You looked at our membership rolls?"

"Is that a problem?" ban Wyvald asked.

"That is an invasion of our privacy!"

Tresyllione smiled again, and Boslin rather wished she hadn't. "Your membership dues payments are registered with the tax office. Those records are publicly available to anyone in the lord and lady's government who requests them—and the Castle Guard is a part of the lord and lady's government."

Boslin found he had nothing to say to that.

"In any event," ban Wyvald said, "we noticed that one of your members is Trethen lothHratha."

"Yes? So? Trethen hates wizards, same as us."

"Were you aware that she also was incarcerated?"

Boslin swallowed. "I'd heard a rumor to that effect. She wasn't at our last meeting, and people gossiped, though I didn't put much stock in it."

"So, you're unaware," ban Wyvald said, "that your pageboy, Willard, visited her in the hole?"

Tresyllione shook her head. "Willard does *love* to visit prisoners, doesn't he?"

Choosing his words carefully, Boslin said, "I didn't wish to speak of this in public, but I suppose it doesn't matter—as a fellow member of FAW, we offered to pay her debts while she was in prison. Her sister died, leaving her with—"

"Yes, we're aware of her financial situation," Tresyllione said, "including that you paid her debts—in exchange for her killing Sozin."

"I'm sorry? What's a Sozin?" This time, Boslin thought he sounded more convincing.

"Sozin," ban Wyvald said, "is the person you had pay off Quolt and his friends to assault various random Barlin refugees in order to cover up the fact that you wanted them to kill Gedling before he revealed your allegiance to the Cabal for a Better Flingaria. You then paid Trethen to kill Sozin so he wouldn't talk, either."

"That's—that's absurd! I told you, Trethen had debts, and as fellow—"

"Please, stop," Tresyllione said. "You already incriminated yourself when you mentioned Gedling overhearing things—something you never mentioned before."

"I told you, that was just personal—"

"And then," Tresyllione said, "there's the matter of the statement that was made by Sozin's employer."

Boslin blinked. "I'm sorry?"

"Sozin worked for Jerri Donoh," ban Wyvald said.

Tresyllione added, "But you already knew that. You knew that Jerri wouldn't have any problem taking money for any task, even if it was assault."

"Though you did need to up the price for murder—from what Jerri said in his statement," ban Wyvald said with a small smile, "he did rather insist on a higher price for killing someone."

Quickly, Boslin tried to come up with some kind of explanation. "I don't know what—"

"Your mistake," Tresyllione interrupted, "in case you were wondering, was in killing Sozin. You see, Jerri is *very* discreet. It was smart to use him to hire those hobgoblin-mask-wearing shitbrains."

Ban Wyvald said, "But Jerri is also very loyal to his employees. He has always treated them fairly."

"Unfortunately," Tresyllione said with a sigh, "it's one of the reasons why we've had such a hard time pinning very many crimes on him. He treats his people well, and they refuse to testify against him, preferring to serve time on the barge rather than give him up."

"That loyalty cuts both ways," ban Wyvald said, "and after his right-hand was killed, he wasted no time in coming to us to aid in our investigation into Sozin's death."

"I have to give you credit," Tresyllione said, "I didn't think *anything* would get Jerri to talk to us willingly, but apparently needlessly murdering one of his most valuable employees did it."

Boslin just sat in the chair, listening to the two detectives carry on.

They knew all along. The revelation had finally hit him at some point when ban Wyvald and Tresyllione were carrying on about Jerri Donoh. They'd already talked to Donoh, and to Trethen, and looked at their tax records, and their membership listings, and the list of people who'd visited Trethen in prison—all before they sent that guard to fetch Boslin from the mansion.

"Very well," he said quietly.

"I'm sorry?" Tresyllione asked.

"Very well what?" ban Wyvald prompted.

Letting out a long sigh, Boslin said, "Yes, Elmira and I are part of the Cabal for a Better Flingaria. Willard went to visit Voran in his cell to remind him of the importance of not talking about the cabal or revealing any of its membership to the Castle Guard."

Tresyllione snorted. "Threatening someone who was already condemned to boil in oil. That's rather ballsy."

"He killed the queen's sister!" Boslin threw up his hands. "That was the other thing we told Willard to pass on to him, that he was a complete imbecile! The whole *point* of the exercise was to enact a peaceful transition of power from Queen Marta to the Pirate Queen. If she said no—which we *always* knew was a possibility—we would move on to a *different* plan! Voran endangered the entire organization with his murderous behavior, and Willard's message was to remind him not to endanger it any more than he already had."

Amazingly, Boslin felt more relaxed than he had since — well, since he'd first found out that Voran had killed the Pirate Queen, truthfully. All the lies and the cover-ups and whatnot had been wearing.

Ban Wyvald asked, "Do you admit to paying Sozin to attack Barlin refugees?"

Boslin scoffed. "Would there be any point to denying it?" He sighed. "Yes. Gedling overheard Elmira and I discussing cabal business, and he started blackmailing us. He was bleeding us dry, and there was no guarantee that he wouldn't still turn us in."

"So you had him killed?" Tresyllione said.

"It was the only way to be rid of him. It was Elmira's idea to have other *bahrlans* targeted first, so you people would think it was just the latest attack in a series."

Getting to his feet, ban Wyvald said, "Boslin Fansarri, you are under arrest for conspiracy to commit murder."

Pulling Boslin to his feet, ban Wyvald then led Boslin out into the squadroom.

To Boslin's horror, Lord Doval was standing there with Captain Dru. His lordship was staring angrily ahead with his arms folded, glowering at Boslin.

Dru asked, "He confessed?"

"He did," Tresyllione said. "He's part of the same cabal that killed the Pirate Queen — and, probably, also killed Lord Albin and tried to kill the king and queen."

That brought Boslin up short. It seemed the Castle Guard knew even more than he realized…

"I am appalled and disgusted," Lord Doval said. "I assume Elmira will also be arrested?"

"Yes," Tresyllione said. "We thought interrogating the husband would go more smoothly than the wife."

Boslin couldn't help but chuckle at their perspicacity. Getting a word in with Elmira was damn near impossible.

And Boslin dug his own grave, anyhow.

"Take him away from my sight, please," Doval said through clenched teeth.

The same guard who had escorted him from his home to the castle was standing nearby, and Dru looked at him and said, "Bonce, take Sir Boslin down to the hole, then take a couple guards to the Fansarri mansion and bring Madam Elmira and that pageboy, what's-his-name?"

"Willard," ban Wyvald said.

"Right, Willard."

"Will do, Cap'n," Bonce said as ban Wyvald handed him over.

As Bonce led Boslin out of the squadroom, he wondered where, exactly, he went wrong. *Maybe we should've just kept paying Gedling...*

TWENTY-THREE

Captain Dru entered the Lord and Lady's dining room salivating over the smell of the sausages, which this week seemed to have more sage in them.

Look at me, I'm turning into an epicure, he thought with a smile as he took his seat across from Lord Doval.

Doval regarded Dru quizzically as he sat down. "Your beard looks different."

"Yeah, I trimmed it." Dru chuckled. "Was startin' to look like a bird's nest."

"It seems yours looks more like Lieutenant ban Wyvald's."

"Well, not so much anymore," Dru said as he speared the wheatcakes the chef had prepared. "Torin's growin' his full beard back."

"Really? What brought that on?"

"He, uh, ain't datin' the guy who asked him to shave it no more." Dru considered elaborating, but decided against it. He didn't really want his lordship to know that one of his detectives had been lovers with one of the four people who were just hanged yesterday for murdering a Barlin refugee. That's the sort of thing that can cause a boss to lose faith in your employees.

"I see from the reports from the last week that attacks on refugees are down."

"Yeah, once word got out that the guys in hobgoblin masks were bein' paid by aristocrats tryin'a cover up their treason, I'm guessin' people lost their taste for bein' shitbrains toward refugees."

"Let's hope it's the start of a trend, and not a blip because of distaste for the hobgoblin mask wearers." Doval sighed. "I had hoped that taking on the refugees from Barlin would be seen as a high point of my time in charge of the city-state, but the more attacks there are, the more I fear it will be remembered as a massive mistake."

"I don't think it will be, m'lord," Dru said after swallowing some wheatcake. "I remember after the elven wars ended, we had a mess'a people comin' into Cliff's End, too, comin' home from the war, not to mention a lotta elves who were in even worse shape than the folks from Barlin. Pissed off a lotta people to start, an' there was some violence then, too, but it all evened out. This is a little worse 'cause they all came in at once, and most of 'em are livin' in New Ba— Uh, in Albinton, but still, I think it'll be okay. Just give it time."

Doval chuckled. "It's quite all right, Captain, you can call it New Barlin if you wish. I appear to have lost that particular fight. In any event, I hope your optimism is warranted."

"Me, too, m'lord."

"Also, I have news from my mother, one good, one bad."

Dru almost choked on his sausage, and did cough twice, but got himself under control. He already knew what the good news was, and he had a feeling that the "bad" news was nothing but.

"First the good news: she has approved the notion of hiring two more detectives. Apparently, there's quite the budget surplus."

"That *is* good news, m'lord, thank you!"

"I'll leave it to you to decide which two guards or sergeants should be promoted."

That brought Dru up short. "Sergeants?"

"Well, yes, of course. After all, lieutenant is a promotion from sergeant, and I imagine that at least some of the sergeants might make good detectives."

Dru rubbed his newly trimmed beard. Lieutenants were almost always taken from the guard ranks—as were sergeants. Because their duties were administrative, the guards who were groomed for detective work were rarely the same as those who were groomed for running a precinct shift. "Interesting. I'll have to go through the roster. What's the bad news?"

"My mother has insisted that Ankh Security be allowed to reopen."

"I see," Dru said neutrally.

"In truth, I see her argument. But I consider it bad news because you came to me with insufficient information."

Dru picked his next words very carefully. "It was the information we had. Look, I agree, it woulda been nice if Aleta an' Dannee had more to go on when I came to you, but they were already workin' another case. See this is *why* I've been askin' for more detectives. The six we got have *way* too much to deal with as it is. Stuff is gettin' missed."

"I do see the point. In any event, Mr. Wirrn may reopen his business and continue protecting the merchants of Jorbin's Way. I still think that this is a waste of time, but Mother's arguments were actually rather convincing."

Dru nodded and covered a smile by putting more wheatcakes in his mouth. The arguments were the ones that Danthres, Aleta, and Dannee themselves made to her ladyship, so he was quite content with that.

They continued to talk about various other matters while they each ate their wheatcakes and sausage. Once he was done, Dru excused himself and got to his feet.

"Oh, Captain?" Doval said as Dru started to push his chair in.

"Yeah, m'lord?"

"I'm impressed with how you handled the Fansarris. I must confess, I did not expect that. You could also have easily made a spectacle of them, but you dealt with the matter discreetly."

Recalling how Elmira Fansarri had reacted to being arrested, Dru said, "Well, I did the best I could under the circumstances."

"The point, Captain, is that you made the effort. Whatever public scandal will befall those two is entirely their own doing. The Castle Guard worked to mitigate the damage, and that is the sort of thing that is appreciated by the people in the western wing."

"My pleasure, m'lord." And with that, Dru gave a small bow, and then turned and headed back to the squadroom.

Jonas was there, of course, as were Danthres, Aleta, Manfred, Kellan, and Dannee. It was already an hour past the start of shift. "Torin *still* ain't here? This is bad even by his standards."

Danthres shook her head. "He asked for the day off. Watching Jak get hanged yesterday was a bit much for him."

Dru winced. "He went to the hanging?"

Holding up both hands, Danthres said, "I *told* him not to! I threatened to tie him down to his bed so he wouldn't go, and in retrospect, I should've made good on that threat."

"Yeah, you should've." Dru sighed. "All right, well, anyhow, Lord Doval gave us the official okay to hire two more detectives. Jonas, I need you to arrange to get a couple more desks in here."

"Who's getting promoted?" Aleta asked.

"Well, we only get two, so we gotta make sure we pick the right ones. But I wanted to ask you guys."

"What about Hariella?" Dannee said. "She's always impressed me with her brilliance. I think she'd make an excellent detective."

Kellan laughed. "That means she's gotta come out in daylight. Never happen. How about Jared?"

"Please," Manfred said, "he's always makin' fun of us."

"Yeah, an' you used t'make fun right with him back when you were a guard. If that don't disqualify you, it don't disqualify him, neither."

"I think Simon's a better bet," Manfred said.

Aleta said, "I agree with all three choices."

Regarding Danthres quizzically, Dru asked, "What about you?"

"I agree with none of the choices. But I think all the guards are shitbrained morons, so I'm not the best person to ask."

"Yeah," Kellan said with a chuckle, "she was always callin' us shitbrained morons when we were guards."

Smiling sweetly, Danthres asked, "For what possible reason, Kellan, are you using the *past* tense there?"

"Hardy har har."

"I'm not kidding."

"Yes, she is," Dru said quickly, "because if she wasn't, she'd also have t'admit that she still thinks her captain is a shitbrained moron, and Danthres ain't *that* dumb, right?"

"Absolutely not," Danthres said in as unconvincing a tone as Dru had ever heard her use.

Deciding to settle for that insincere declaration, he then recalled what Lord Doval had said and asked, "What about some of the sergeants?"

"Not me," Jonas said emphatically. "I had enough of investigations with that Hamnau gem ridiculousness."

Dru nodded in sympathy. A couple of years ago, a killer had used a Hamnau gem to possess other people and commit murders—one of them was Jonas. It had been very traumatic for him.

"Actually, that's not a bad idea," Danthres said, "as long as you don't consider Slaney. But Kaplan has something approaching brain cells."

"So does Mannit," Aleta said.

"Not Kaplan," Dru said. "He only just got promoted to sergeant, and besides, we need 'im in Phoenix to make up for Slaney bein' a disaster."

"Can't you just fire Slaney?" Danthres asked plaintively.

"Not unless you can use chronotic magick to go back to midsummer an' stop him from savin' the Wint kid." Dru rubbed his trimmed beard. "Mannit's not a bad idea, though. Only problem is, who do we put in charge'a Mermaid, then? Same problem as Kaplan, he's got that place runnin' smooth, finally."

Aleta said, "It's not just Mannit. Shreth lothHeshral has been doing an excellent job running the night-shift."

"That's it!" Dannee said.

Dru turned to her. "What's it?"

"Promote Sergeant Mannit to lieutenant, put Sergeant lothHeshral in charge of the day shift, and promote Hariella to sergeant and put her in charge of Mermaid's night shift!"

Manfred stared at her. "I thought you said she'd make a good detective."

"She would. But she'd also make a good sergeant, and she'll actually take a night-shift job."

Dru considered it. "Depends on whether or not Mannit even *wants* the job. I mean, he ain't gettin' any younger."

Aleta said, "And he came out of retirement when Captain Osric asked him to run Mermaid because he was bored to death. I think he'll like the challenge."

"What about Afrak?" Manfred asked. "He always seems to know everybody and everything."

Danthres said, "Of all the guards at the scene at the boulder, he was the only one who knew who Tuchera even *was*. But he's also a shit-brained moron of the highest order — and not just because he's a guard. He's friends with *Nulti*."

Dru sighed. Too many good choices, and too many problems with each of them. Afrak was indeed a decent choice, and Dru didn't want to not promote someone based on who their friends were. On the other hand, Nulti really was garbage — too stupid to be any good at his job, too incompetent at his meagre corruption to even be fired. Besides which, Nulti was still assigned to Goblin, while Afrak was now working Phoenix.

"All right, I'll think about this and start talkin' to some'a the candidates." He sighed. "Meantime, Aleta, Dannee, you two get down to Rob Wirrn's place an' tell him he can reopen Ankh Security."

"Excellent!" Dannee cried out. "Thank you *so* much, Captain!"

"Hey, thank you for talkin' to Lady Meerka. That's what did the trick."

Dru went into his office, and sat down at his desk. Attacks on refugees were down, the Fansarris were arrested, the hobgoblin mask killers were hanged, and he was getting two more detectives. And on top of that, the lord of the demesne paid him a sincere compliment.

I may not suck too badly at this job…

DOVAL WAS RATHER SURPRISED TO FIND HIS SISTER JULIANA WAITING FOR HIM in his office when he returned from his breakfast with Captain Dru. Tall and lanky, his sister leaned against the wall, but stood up straight to her considerable height—nearly half a head taller than Doval himself—upon his entrance.

"Juliana? What are you—? How did you—?"

Rolling her eyes, Juliana said, "Oh, do stop stammering, Doval, it's unseemly. I got Hanlii to use a Teleport Spell. He owns one of the magick shops here in Cliff's End, so he's going to inspect it, make sure all is well, then take me back with him. No one will know I'm here besides you and your secretary, who I assume is discreet?"

"Of course," Doval said absently. Taja was completely trustworthy. "But I don't understand, why are you here in secret?"

"To find out what in the *hell* you're playing at here! Elmira and Boslin have been *arrested*? Couldn't you *do* something about that?"

"What, pray tell, was I to do?"

"Stop it from happening! You *are* the lord of the demesne, aren't you?"

Doval sighed and sat down at his desk. "In order to do something about it, I would have had to contrive a way for the Castle Guard not to find out that those two imbeciles hired thugs to kill a landscaper—well, in fact, two landscapers, as the thugs killed the wrong one the first time."

"Why are they taking out murder contracts on landscapers?"

"Apparently one overheard them speaking of the cabal and was blackmailing them. So they took steps to rectify the situation—and every single step turned into a stumble. In truth, Juliana, I believe that removing those two from the field of play can only benefit us, given their spectacular incompetence."

"They followed instructions and have a great deal of money," Juliana said. "Damn the Castle Guard anyhow. Perhaps you should have continued Blayk's endeavor to move them away from their policing function and back into a proper army."

"No," Doval said emphatically.

"Don't take that tone with me," Juliana said, "it's a reasonable suggestion!"

"No, it isn't!" Doval sighed. "For starters, the refugee situation has barely been contained, and that only because the Castle Guard is performing its policing function. Can you imagine what Iaron would be like with this type of influx of people?"

Juliana visibly shuddered, which answered Doval's question.

"Besides," Doval continued, "ban Wyvald and Tresyllione are practically folk heroes after solving Gan Brightblade *and* the Pirate Queen's murders. Plus they are favorites of Marcus and Marta."

"How did two filthy guards contrive to become favorites of the Silver Thrones?" Juliana asked incredulously.

"Do you not read my letters? They're the ones who found Blayk out, and on top of that, they were the ones who found Voran out."

"Oh. For some reason, I assumed that your references to a Danthres Tresyllione and a Torin ban Wyvald were two of the nobility."

Now it was Doval's turn to roll his eyes at his sister. "Hardly, though I suppose ban Wyvald is considered nobility in Myverin. Nonetheless, in addition to everything I've mentioned, tourism is up considerably, and it's at least in part thanks to the Castle Guard. No, they must stay as they are, at least for the time being."

Raising an eyebrow, Juliana said, "Oh?"

"A protection service has started. I believe that, long-term, we can shift the Castle Guard's policing functions to them, and, slowly, have the Castle Guard once again become a standing army."

Nodding, Juliana said, "Mmm. Clever, little brother."

"Oh, don't call me that, I'm still two years older than you."

"Perhaps, but you'll always be two hands shorter."

"Is there anything else?"

Juliana sighed. "I suppose not. I'm just tired of all these setbacks. First Blayk killing Father and rushing the plan, then the fire in Barlin, then Voran botching things with the Pirate Queen, and now the Fansarris."

"That's all they are — setbacks. The plan is still in place and moving forward, and no one is on to us. We'll be all right."

"I hope so," Juliana said gravely.

Torin ban Wyvald lay on his bed, staring at the ceiling.

He hadn't really moved from that spot except to relieve himself and to drink water. He hadn't eaten anything all day, as his growling stomach reminded him, and he thought about getting out of bed and going to get some food.

However, he did not marry that thought to an action, instead continuing to stare at the ceiling.

Then he heard the door lock click. Which meant that someone was using their key to enter.

Well, no, not "someone." Only three people had a key to these apartments: his landlady, himself, and Danthres.

Sure enough, Danthres walked in. "Torin?"

"In the bedroom."

Danthres came into the bedroom and saw Torin laying on the bed. "How are you doing?"

"I have been better."

"Well, get up, you need to come get drunk."

"I really do not wish to, Danthres."

"Have you gotten up from that bed all day?"

"Once or twice."

"Well, you're getting up now."

"I *really* do not wish to."

Danthres sat on the edge of the bed. "You can't just lay here. Manfred, Kellan, Dannee, Dru, and the Shranlaseth are at the Chain, and you need to join us so we can celebrate."

"What, precisely, are we celebrating?"

"Quite a bit, actually." Danthres proceeded to tell him about Lord Doval and Lady Meerka agreeing to hire two more detectives and to reopen Ankh Security. "Oh, plus we arrested some aristocrats, which is always worth celebrating."

"And I got to watch the man I love get hanged."

With a sigh, Danthres put a hand on his. "All the more reason to go out with your workmates and get drunk."

"I haven't eaten anything all day. And Urgoss hasn't created a kitchen."

"Fine, we'll stop by that cart you like on Cobble Path and grab a bowl of stew before we go to the Chain."

"I really do not—"

Now Danthres tightened her grip on Torin's hand. "If you say you don't wish to one more time, I'll break your fingers."

"I just—" Torin let out a very long sigh. "I don't know what to do, Danthres."

"Move on. You fell in love with a murderer, and as an added bonus, you got to arrest him, and then you rather stupidly watched him die. Your options now going forward are to move on or to wallow in self-pity. Personally, I find wallowing to be a waste of time and energy. And you know what? So do you."

Torin sighed. "I just—" he started again, and then laughed at the repetition. "I don't know what I did wrong."

"Ah, see, that's your problem. You didn't do a thing wrong. You can't help who you fall in love with. You can only help what you do about it. And what you did about it was arrest the person you love once you found out he was a murdering piece of slime." She leaned forward. "And by the way? That was an incredibly brave thing that you didn't even have to do. I could easily have made the arrest myself, but you confronted him rather than back away from it."

"Yes, and he tried to blame me for betraying him, as if it were that, and not the other way 'round." Torin sighed and then sat up. "I suppose I should eat something."

"And then drink several somethings. Come on." She got up from the bed and tugged on Torin's arm.

After a moment, and a laugh, he allowed her to pull him off the bed. He stood alongside it for a second, and then looked down at the wrinkled bedclothes he was wearing. "I'd best change."

Grinning, Danthres said, "Probably a good idea, yes."

As he shrugged out of his nightshirt, Torin said, "Thank you for coming to get me, Danthres."

"Always, partner. You've done the same for me, and no doubt will again."

"As I'm sure you will for me." Torin smiled at her. "And at least now I can grow the beard back."

"Why did you shave it down?"

Torin sighed. "Jak didn't like kissing me with it, and I liked kissing him. He was an excellent kisser." He climbed into a pair of pantaloons and found a shirt to wear. "All right, let's line my stomach and then get me exceedingly drunk."

"Good plan." Danthres headed toward the door.

Following her, Torin said, "And Danthres?"

"Yes?"

"Can we end the evening at your place? I need to stay away from these apartments for a bit."

"Of course," Danthres said.

"I doubt I'll be up for much more than sleeping."

"I doubt you'll be conscious with all the ale we plan to pour down your throat," Danthres said with a laugh.

"Excellent."

And so, they went out together.

BONUS VIGNETTES

Starting in December 2017, I started a Patreon (patreon.com/krad), which includes — among other things — monthly vignettes featuring my original characters, including those from the "Precinct" series.

As an added bonus here in Phoenix Precinct, here are, for the first time outside the Patreon, nine of those vignettes.

The Banishment of Helsek Gam

This tale from Flingaria's ancient past is about the dragonriders who fought against an evil wizard, as mentioned in Phoenix Precinct, *and also in the short story "Fire in the Hole."*

THE SORFAR CHARGED.

Gamtar sat between the wings of Niannto, his dragon. With his thoughts, he guided Niannto toward the form of Helsek Gam, currently standing on the coastline of the Garamin Sea. The evil wizard was attempting to take over the Redoubt at the End of the Cliffs, one of the castles that defended the territory of Syleen the Weary. Indeed, it was the most critical of those castles, as sat overlooking the Garamin as well as the natural port formed by the coastline as it was right in the middle of the transition from sheer cliffs to the northeast into beachfronts to the southwest. But here, it was a natural port, which made the redoubt one of the most important in Syleen's kingdom.

Which was why Helsek Gam wanted to take it.

The four dragons that made up the Sorfar had flown here from Syleen's throne in the Redoubt at the Barlin River. Niannto and Gamtar were part of the two teams of dragonrider and dragon who attacked physically, distracting Helsek Gam and keeping him from advancing inward from the sea.

Niannto flew high and far at Gamtar's mental urging, and then dove toward Helsek Gam, who was busy trying to use his magicks to swat Lekym aside, though Lekym's rider kept her steady.

Even as Niannto and Lekym flit about, attacking from above and to the side, the other two dragons were doing their own work.

Mozprof was flying to different spots on the ground between the sea and the redoubt to place runestones.

Once they were in place, Inmari, the rider atop Uratmep would finish the spell she was in the midst of preparing. She had gathered the components, and awaited Mozprof completing the placement of the runes.

Suddenly, Helsek Gam gestured grandly, and lightning crashed down from the clear blue sky and struck both Niannto and Lekym. Gamtar felt the pain of the electricity coursing through Niannto's scales through their link, and the dragon started to plummet downward toward the sea.

Pull up! Gamtar urged. *Pull up!*

But he felt nothing from Niannto in reply.

Niannto had still been rather high in the air when the lightning struck, but Lykem had been closer to the evil wizard's head, and plummeted directly into the Garamin Sea.

Just as Niannto was about to do likewise, he suddenly awoke and spread his golden wings, soaring back into the air.

Letting out a vicious war cry, Niannto flew directly at Helsek Gam and breathed a massive exhalation of fire at the wizard.

While their foe was able to erect a magickal shield against the fire, it also provided cover for Gamtar to try a more mundane approach. Notching an arrow into his bow, he let loose with the small wooden missile, hoping it could sneak in through Helsek Gam's defenses.

At that, it succeeded, at least in the abstract. The arrow sliced into the wizard's leg, and Helsek Gam let out a mighty cry.

"You will rue this day, dragonriders!" the wizard called out and then summoned more lightning, this one striking Mozprof and his rider. While the rider fell to the ground, Mozprof remained airborne and kept his grip on the runestones. Knowing that the mission was more important than a single life, the dragon flew onward, placing the last of the runestones.

Needing to get Helsek Gam's attention on himself rather than on Inmari, who was casting the banishment spell that would activate the runestones, Gamtar cried out, "It is you will be doing the ruing, mage!"

"Three of your precious Sorfar are already dead, dragonrider," Helsek Gam said with a sneer.

Gamtar tried not to think about those words. He only had the wizard's word for it that Mozprof's rider, Lykem, and Lykem's rider had perished.

And even if they had, they had pledged to give their lives to defend the throne.

Helsek Gam continued, "And you will follow them into oblivion!"

Grinning, as he saw Inmari sprinkle the herbs into the pestle, which he knew was the final step of the spell, Gamtar said, "You first."

The runestones all began to glow. Arranged in the pattern of one of the oldest of the mystic sigils, light shot forth from each of them straight into the air above. The beams of light then formed a canopy over the entire tableau.

And then the light struck Helsek Gam.

The wizard screamed in agony and then disappeared a moment later.

Inmari collapsed atop the dragon's back. The banishment spell was a powerful one, and Gamtar wondered if she would be able to properly recover from casting it.

But it was done. Helsek Gam was banished to a netherworld. Syleen the Weary's rule was safe for another day. Many more days, in truth, for few had menaced them as much as the evil wizard.

Gamtar cast his mind to his mental link to Niannto and said, *We have done well today, my dragon.*

Yes, we have, Niannto thought in return, *but I mourn the loss of our brothers and sisters.*

As do I, old friend. But our work is not yet done. Inmari told us that we must be vigilant and inspect the runestones regularly. This means I must now charge you with an all-important task.

The honor is to serve, Niannto thought with pride.

Every midsummer, you will return to the Redoubt at the End of the Cliffs and inspect the runestones. Every midwinter, Mozprof will do the same. We will not allow Helsek Gam to return.

It will be done.

Gamtar felt the determination in Niannto. He would return every midsummer and make sure that the spell that kept Helsek Gam banished would remain intact, thus keeping Flingaria in general and Syleen's kingdom in particular safe forevermore.

For that was the Sorfar's duty.

On a Cold Winter's Night

This tale takes place during the elven wars, when Torin ban Wyvald served as a soldier under General Osric, about fifteen years prior to Phoenix Precinct.

"MITRE'S BONES, IT'S COLD."

Corporal Torin ban Wyvald heard those words come from General Osric's tent as he passed by. He was heading to his own tent in the Nemerian Wastes, trudging through the snow after having finished his patrol for the night.

Deciding to see if he could help, he poked his head inside. Osric was there along with his batman.

"Are you all right, General?"

Osric looked up and stared at him with his steely eyes. "Merely freezing my ass off, ban Wyvald, same as everyone. Don't know how I'm going to sleep in this."

"Might I make a suggestion, sir?"

"I hope this isn't another of your words of wisdom from the collegium in Myverin," Osric said with a scowl.

Chuckling, Torin said, "Not at all, sir—rather words of wisdom that came from spending my first winter after leaving Myverin in the Forest of Orven."

Osric blinked. "You spent a winter in Orven?"

"Yes, sir."

"Only a complete imbecile spends a winter in Orven."

"Yes, sir."

"You never struck me as a complete imbecile, ban Wyvald."

"No, sir, but I knew nothing of the Forest of Orven prior to my traversing it that winter. I knew nothing of the world outside Myverin."

The batman was staring at Torin wide-eyed. "How did you survive?"

"Barely," Torin said with a rueful smile.

Unbidden, memories came crashing down in his mind like waves — or like the snow that had flurried about earlier that day, rendering their battle plans moot.

He remembered slipping and straining his shoulder, making his right arm useless for a week.

He remembered not realizing he was walking across ice until it collapsed underneath his feet and he plunged into freezing water.

He remembered his beloved horse, Sylvan Wye, freezing to death.

That had been the hardest thing. Sylvan Wye had been his faithful companion since he was a boy, and the only part of Myverin he wished to bring with him into the greater world of Flingaria. The poor steed got to see so very little of that outside world.

Casting the memories aside, Torin gave a more proper response to the batman's question: "One way I managed at night was to strip myself naked before going to bed and wrap myself in furs and blankets."

Osric scoffed. "Why would I remove clothes in order to stay warmer?"

"The body generates heat, sir. But if you lay down in the same armor you wore in the winter weather all day, it will hold in the cold it has absorbed. But if you remove the armor and allow your body heat to radiate out into the area held in by your blankets, you will keep much warmer."

"If you say so."

"It is the only reason I survived Orven, sir."

"Very well. Thank you. Is there anything else?"

"No, sir, I'm just coming off patrol. There's been no sign of the enemy — likely they're also hunkered down in their own tents."

"No doubt. Get some sleep, ban Wyvald. We'll speak in the morning."

"Yes, sir."

As he left, Torin heard the batman say, "Strip oneself naked. Never heard such rubbish. I thought they were *smart* in Myverin."

"They are," Osric replied, "which is why I'm going to try what the corporal suggests."

Smiling, Torin continued back to his tent.

Silly Season

This takes place the first winter after Torin joined the Castle Guard, about eleven years prior to Phoenix Precinct.

"ALL RIGHT, WE'VE GOTTEN THE FIRST SNOWFALL, SO OUR SILLY SEASON HAS begun," Sergeant Newcastle said as he looked out at four of the detectives of the Cliff's End Castle Guard on this cold morning. The other two members of the squad were out sick with winter colds.

The newest of the detectives, Lieutenant Torin ban Wyvald, who had only been on the job for a few months, looked confused. "Silly season?"

Lieutenant Linder said, "It's when we start celebrating all the new years."

"All five hundred of them," Linder's partner Lieutenant Iaian muttered.

"I'm sorry? I thought here in King Marcus and Queen Marta's lands, the new year was celebrated at the end of winter?"

"That's one of 'em, yeah," Iaian said with a laugh. "King and Queen are Temisa worshippers, so they go with her way."

"Don't forget, ban Wyvald here has only been in Cliff's End a few months, and before that, he fought with Osric in the war," said Lieutenant Danthres Tresyllione. Torin was the half-elf woman's partner, a position Torin had held longer than anyone since Danthres was promoted to lieutenant.

"Let me guess," Linder said, "in the trenches, the only holidays were the Temisan ones?"

Torin nodded. "It was a surprise to me, as in Myverin, we did not have an annual calendar. We simply observed the passage of time by the waxing and waning of the moon. I'd never even heard of the concept of numbering the years until I joined the army."

"The elves are the same way," Danthres said.

Newcastle chuckled. "Well, we've got a whole bunch of different ways of numbering the years, and the first one is usually whenever we get our first snowfall."

"First snowfall?" Torin asked.

"The dwarves believe that Xinf created the world in winter, so as far as they're concerned, the year starts when winter starts," Newcastle said.

Linder said, "Then you've got Mitre, who says the new year starts at midwinter."

Danthres added, "The gnomes don't start their new year until the first thaw, as their Demiurge allegedly started the calendar by making the world warm."

"Wiate's smart," Iaian said. "He says the year starts at the solstice when the days get longer again."

Torin rubbed his bearded chin. "That makes a certain sense. The sun renewing itself is very symbolic."

Iaian stared at him. "Huh?"

"As the days get longer, it can be viewed as the sun restoring itself to life. It's an excellent reason to celebrate."

"Well," Newcastle said, "most folks find a reason to celebrate, and since no one agrees when the new year starts, they all celebrate at different times. Which, in practical terms, means we'll have about two months' worth of drunk-and-disorderlies, property damage, brawls, and any number of other idiocies. Starting tonight with the dwarves."

Frowning, Torin asked, "What of Ghandurha?"

Newcastle asked, "What of him?"

"When do his worshippers celebrate the new year?"

Linder snorted. "Those shit-suckers don't celebrate anything. Might lead to fornicating, so they don't party for no reason."

"Thank Wiate we don't have any of them in the Guard," Iaian muttered.

One of the Guards came into the squadroom. "We got a buncha dwarves settin' fire to one'a the boats onna docks!"

"And so it begins..." Newcastle muttered. "Iaian, Linder, you're up next."

"To do what?" Linder asked. "We ain't the fire brigade."

"Find out who did it," the sergeant said, "and arrest them."

"Joy," Iaian muttered.

Another Guard came in. "Two dwarves and an elf got into a fight on Meerka Way."

Newcastle looked at Torin and Danthres.

Torin smiled. "And so it continues?"

"Get used to it, ban Wyvald," Danthres said. "This is what your life will be until spring."

Sisters Need Not Apply

This story serves as a prequel to Goblin Precinct, *showing Morenn's early days trying to be a wizard.*

MORENN FOCUSED HER MIND, AND SPOKE THE WORDS SHE'D FOUND IN THE old tomes in the Royal Library.

She dropped the herbs into the pestle, then spoke the final word of the spell —

— and nothing happened.

"Dammit!"

She'd managed so many other spells, from Inanimate Residue to Open Door to Color Change. But she still hadn't quite nailed Teleport.

She forced herself to remember the words Brother Genero spoke to her. "Calm is the key, Morenn. You must remove the anger, tamp down the frustration, and achieve equanimity. Temisa only gifts those who are not distracted."

Of course, as far as Morenn was concerned, Temisa had nothing to do with it, but Genero was a Temisan priest, so invoking her was an occupational hazard.

And, damn him, he'd been right. When she calmed herself, the magick came more easily.

If only it had been enough to convince Vastar.

The local Brotherhood of Wizards representative, Morenn had gone to him on Brother Genero's advice, after both he and the Temisan monks who'd raised Morenn in the orphanage found her too talented a mage for them to handle.

She had made the journey on foot to Vastar's mansion, located on a high hill, and had pounded on the front door.

It had opened without a person on the other side, which Morenn had assumed was accomplished by magick. A glowing ball of light had then led her to Vastar's office.

"What is it you want that you have chosen to invade my home?"

Morenn had frowned. "I'm not invading, I'm requesting an audience. If I was invading, I wouldn't have knocked."

"Please cease quibbling over semantics and come to the point of your visit."

"I wish to be trained in the use of magick. I already have some skills, and—"

"Women cannot wield magick."

A moment later, Morenn had found herself back in Velessa. Vastar had teleported her into the middle of town, and she had been forced to walk home.

She focused her mind again, and once again spoke the words to the Teleport Spell.

Once again, nothing happened.

She threw the pestle across the room, and it clattered against the wall.

"You must remove the anger."

Easy for you to say, Brother, she thought as she went to pick the pestle up off the floor.

She had returned to Vastar's mansion the following day, this time bringing the pestle and spell components for Color Change. She had altered the hue of Vastar's desk from brown to green and his robes from purple to bright yellow.

Vastar had been less than impressed. "Anyone may purchase a spell and pretend to cast it. I say again that women cannot wield magick. Begone."

The third and fourth times, he wouldn't even talk to her, even though she cast a Fireball on his fireplace. (She didn't wish to actually burn the place down, as that was counterindicated to what she wished to accomplish. It was going to be hard enough to convince the Brotherhood of Wizards to train her, but that difficulty would increase a thousandfold if she burned down a wizard's house. Though she was tempted.)

So she was determined to prove her worth by teleporting into the mansion. Teleport Spells could not be purchased, so his idiotic argument that she was faking it wouldn't fly.

Besides, what did she have to gain by pretending to be a wizard? It wasn't like it was *easy*.

It wasn't like she could do anything else, either. Magick flowed through her body like blood. Not being a mage was like not being alive — she couldn't conceive of it, couldn't even discuss it.

But she needed training.

She was *going* to master this spell.

Maybe it's time I ignored Brother Genero's advice, she thought.

Instead of removing her anger, she embraced it. She thought about Vastar's arrogant face and how very much she wanted to punch it. She thought about Brother Genero's tiresome overprotectiveness and frustrated it made her. She thought about the other orphans at the monastery who taunted her for wanting to be a mage, parroting Vastar's tired line about how women couldn't be wizards.

She'd already proven them *all* wrong. She *was* a wizard. They could call it the "Brotherhood of Wizards" all they wanted, they could make all the declarations they wanted, but she could wield magick as well as any man.

And the best way to convince Vastar was to cast a spell that couldn't be purchased.

Her mind filled with righteous anger and furious indignation, she spoke the words and put the herbs in the pestle.

A flash of light, and she was standing in her back yard.

Pumping her fist, she cried out, "Yes! I did it! See, Vastar! See, Genero! I'm a wizard, dammit!"

A voice came from the next house over. "Will you shut up, woman, we're trying to sleep!"

Morenn just laughed more loudly and went back inside on foot.

I'll show you who's a wizard, Vastar. She prepared the spell once again, drawing upon the anger and frustration, and teleported to the wizard's mansion for the final time.

Existential Crisis

This piece was written when I was challenged by Gary Mitchel — podcaster, pop-culture maven, and a track leader at Dragon Con — to write a story about a barbarian having an existential crisis.

GARRI THE BARBARIAN SAT IN THE ROOM BY HIMSELF, PICKING AT A SPLINTER in the wooden table he sat behind. He didn't like it very much, and wanted to leave. But when he tried that, a member of the Castle Guard shoved a sword point in his face. Garri didn't have his axe with him — another member of the Castle Guard took it from him when they brought him here — so he couldn't tell the Guard what for like he wanted to. He might've been able to take the Guard, but he might not have, and it wasn't worth the risk.

Besides, the castle was full of Guards, and they *all* had swords. One of them would probably get lucky.

He just wanted to meet up with Crouh, go out to sea, and track down Myk. Especially after he sent that shitbrain after him in the inn. Garri took care of him, and now he'd take care of Myk.

Two more Guards walked in, except they wore brown cloaks. One was a man, the other a woman, though she was the ugliest woman Garri had ever seen.

"Hello," the man, who had a red beard, said. "I'm Lieutenant Torin ban Wyvald, and this is my partner, Lieutenant Danthres Tresyllione."

"I wanna get outta here," Garri said.

"I'm afraid we can't allow that just yet." As he spoke, Torin took a seat in one of the stools opposite him.

Danthres remained standing and said, "We need you to answer some questions, first."

"Look, I was just mindin' my business and that guy came at me with an axe. What the hell else was I s'posed to do? I was defendin' myself!"

"You say he came at you?" Torin asked.

"Ain't that what I just said?"

"Tell us what happened in your own words," Danthres said.

"Whose other words would I use?" Garri shook his head. "Look, I came to Cliff's End to meet up with a friend'a mine."

"And the friend's name?" Torin asked.

"Crouh. He's been here in Cliff's End for a few weeks. Him and me, we was all set to sail down to Dragon Isle. There's a guy there we're lookin' for name'a Myk. Crouh tracked him to Cliff's End, then heard tell that Myk was on Dragon Isle. He sent for me when he found out, and that's where we're goin'."

Danthres asked, "So why didn't you head to the docks?"

"I got down here on my horse, and I put it in one'a the stables, and there was a message from Crouh, and he said to get a room at the Dog an' Duck 'cause our boat ain't ready yet. I thought that was stupid, I can just sleep on the ground like I did on the way down here, but when I got there, Crouh had already gotten a room for me. So I go up, I go lay down, and then somebody knocks on the door, says he's got somethin' for me. I open the door, and there's this guy standin' with an axe. I figure Myk sent this shitbrain to kill me, so I hit him with my axe. Next thing I know, there's six Guards comin' to take me here."

"You did gravely injure someone," Torin said gently.

"I was defendin' myself! When a guy's standin' at your door with an axe, you know damn well what he's there for!"

"Your victim, as it happens, is named Kasenwether. He's a courier, hired by Molano, who's a weaponsmith. He was there to give you the axe."

"Yeah, right inna head!"

"No," Danthres said, "in your hands. Crouh commissioned Molano to craft a new axe for you to use in your campaign against Myk. He wanted it to be a surprise, and he had it delivered to the room he reserved for you."

Then the door opened. A Guard escorted Crouh through it, his arms folded over his bare chest.

Garri stood up. "Crouh? What the hell's goin' on? That axe was for me?"

"Yeah, it was. It was a present."

"Why would you assume that someone who *knocked on your door,*" Danthres said, "would want to kill you?"

"I—" That brought Garri up short. He hadn't thought it through, it was just a guy at the door with an axe. "We don't usually knock on doors where I come from. Shit, we don't *have* doors, mostly."

"I'm afraid we're going to have to imprison you," Torin said, also standing up.

"You mean that guy wasn't gonna kill me?" Garri asked Crouh.

Crouh shook his head. "Nope. It was a gift."

"Shit." Garri's shoulders slumped. His entire world had gone completely askew. How could that guy have been there for any other reason but to kill him?

"Let's go," the Guard who'd led Crouh in said.

"How'm I supposed to go on livin' when I don't even know what the world is even like anymore?"

"You'll get over it," Danthres said, "or you won't. Depending on how the magistrate's feeling, you may not have long to mull it over before you're hanged."

"Shit." Garri allowed the Guard to escort him to the dungeon, despondent.

What even was the world anymore when you can't rely on someone coming at you with an axe to be someone you needed to kill?

Remembrance

This vignette provides some background on Torin's life.

Lieutenant Torin ban Wyvald of the Cliff's End Castle Guard had requested this day off, as he had this day every year since he joined the Castle Guard a decade previous.

He hiked out into the Forest of Nimvale, eventually finding a clearing near a large oak tree. The carving he'd made on this day nine years ago was still on it. It had eroded somewhat, but he could still make out the symbol that was also on the cover of his favorite book.

And under it, written in the language Myverine, the name "Mardeth val Tianni."

His mother.

He gathered branches and rocks and then started a small fire. Once the fire caught, he fell more than sat against the large oak.

And he remembered…

"How was your day, Torin?"

"Fine, Mother. The professor assigned us a reading."

"Of what?"

"She gave us a choice of any book we wish—but once we have read it, we must compose an essay explaining what meaning the book has for us."

"I see."

"There's only one problem."

"What is that, my son?"

"What if the book has no meaning for me?"

"Well, then, we must make sure the book has meaning, won't we?"

"Good evening, my love."

"Good evening, my darling, how was your day as Chief Artisan?"

"Tiresome—the sculptors' proposal went on for hours. How was your day as Council Chef?"

"Uneventful—there were no arcane requests for once, though I am sure that will change as we approach harvest."

"Where is Torin?"

"Reading."

"Is he still reading that ridiculous book?"

"If you mean *Tales of Flingaria,* then yes. It's for an assignment."

"That explains it, then. I wish he'd hurry up and finish it."

"Why is that?"

"Because it's full of nonsense."

"Mother, this book is amazing!"

"I knew you'd like it."

"Are these stories true?"

"I honestly could not say. I can say that they were told by people from all over Flingaria who have visited the Council of Myverin."

"I had no idea there was so much beyond our walls."

"There's an entire world, my son."

"Excuse me, Chief Artisan?"

"Yes?"

"I'm afraid I have some bad news. Council Chef Mardeth has taken ill."

"What happened? She was home!"

"Yes, but the injury she sustained has become infected. She's with a healer and your son now."

"All right. I must finish my work here, but I will be by shortly."

"Mother?"

"I'm here, Torin."

"I—I finished the book this morning, Mother. I was coming to tell you that when I found you on the floor."

"That's wonderful!"

"I was coming to tell you—to tell you that I wanted us to leave Myverin. I want to explore the rest of Flingaria, and see all the sites the book mentions! I want to traipse through the Forest of Orven, sail the Garamin Sea, walk the streets of Cliff's End, explore the caves beneath the Zignat Mountains, view the Nemerian Wastes—there's just so much! And I want you to come with me!"

"I cannot, my son. My duties keep me here."

"They can find another chef to serve the Council. Father could come too—after all, there is no need for a Chief Artisan in these modern times. It's a purely ceremonial duty."

"That's not fair to your father's work—or yours, as it will be one day."

"Not if I leave Myverin."

"Is that your wish, my sweet child?"

"It is, Mother. And I wish you to come with me!"

"When I am well, we will discuss it further."

"I'm sorry, Chief Artisan, Torin—but I'm afraid that Mardeth val Tianni has died."

"What!? But it cannot be! It was a simple infection!"

"There is nothing simple about an infection, Chief Artisan. We were unable to control it, and it spread. I'm sorry."

"No..."

"Father, where are Mother's books?"

"Hm? Oh, I donated them to the collegium library. I saw no reason to keep them around, they simply served as a reminder."

"But I wanted to keep—"

"Do not argue with me, Torin! I did not wish to keep those reminders of her! The books are at the collegium, and if you wish to read them, you may borrow them from there."

"But there was one book that I wished—"

"I asked you not to argue with me, Torin! I will not ask again!"

"Ah, yes, you're ban Wyvald, are you not?"

"Yes, Chief Archivist, and I would like to borrow one of the books. *Tales of Flingaria.*"

"I'm afraid that one is already out. But I will copy down your name and alert you when Solvier val Lorel returns it."

"Thank you, Chief Archivist."

TORIN SAT AT THE OAK TREE FOR HOURS, WATCHING THE FIRE, WHICH eventually died down and cooled to simple embers.

Just like the fire that claimed Solvier val Lorel's home.

While Solvier herself managed to escape the fire, all her possessions were consumed by the flames that resulted from the lightning strike on her house.

In all the years he'd travelled Flingaria—from his time serving in the elven wars to his current job as a lieutenant in the Castle Guard, he had sought out *Tales of Flingaria*, but never found it. Not in his many travels as a soldier, not in Cliff's End, and not in Velessa during his visits there during Lord Blayk's trial.

I lost Mother, and then I lost the book. But I never lost the desire to escape the walls of Myverin.

I just wish I could have taken you with me.

The fire died. Torin stood up.

"Goodbye, Mother. I miss you."

Maternal Day

This is a piece I wrote for Mothers Day.

"AND FINALLY," SERGEANT JONAS SAID, SHUFFLING PARCHMENTS, TO THE squad of detectives in the Cliff's End Castle Guard, "today is Maternal Day for the dwarves, which means we're going to have a *lot* of dwarves taking their mothers out to get drunk all night."

Chuckles and moans went through the squadroom, though Aleta lothLathna made no noise at all, as she was mostly just confused.

After roll call broke up, the detectives went back to sit at their desks.

Lieutenant Manfred shook his head and said, "I hate Maternal Day."

Aleta's partner, the half-dwarf, half-human Lieutenant Dannee Ocly, smiled and said, "I love it!"

Lieutenant Kellan, Manfred's partner, asked, "Ain't your mother the human one?"

"Yes, but she *adores* Maternal Day."

"Besides," Manfred added, "these days, lots of folks are celebrating Maternal Day, not just dwarves."

"That's just odd," Aleta said, shaking her head.

Dannee regarded her quizzically. "What is?"

"We have a Day of Mothers in elf country also. But on that day, we celebrate the children. There's a feast for the all the children that the mothers bore."

"Ah, see, we do that on our birthdays," Kellan said.

Aleta frowned. "That makes no sense. On the anniversary of our birth, we give tribute to our parents. They're the ones whose efforts we should be celebrating that day, not the person who was born."

From his desk, Lieutenant Torin ban Wyvald shook his head. "It has been an endless source of fascination to me how many holidays there are in Flingaria."

Aleta smirked. "No holidays in Myverin?"

"Not as such, no. There were a few anniversaries of historical events that we would acknowledge, but never with such a large celebration as you see here in Cliff's End, or as I saw when I was in the army. And we never celebrated birthdays. Indeed, many people didn't know their exact birth date, as it wasn't a fact of any particular note."

"Well, that sounds boring," Manfred said. "I mean, holidays are a chance to relax, to party, to let out some tension after too many days of working your shitty job."

"Perhaps. And Myverin's boringness is a very large reason why I left. What I find interesting, though, is that there are many celebrations of mothers in several cultures throughout Flingaria, but almost no celebrations of fathers."

Torin's partner, Lieutenant Danthres Tresyllione, said, "Why should there be? The father doesn't actually *do* anything, beyond a single pelvic thrust. The mother then must do all the actual work."

With a musical laugh, Dannee said, "My mother certainly never tires of reminding anyone who'll listen how difficult giving birth to me was."

"That's true of most mothers," Kellan said. "Mine used to tell the story of how she gave birth to me in the middle of making dinner for my father and his coworkers."

Manfred chuckled. "Mine loves telling everyone about how I broke a family heirloom when I was three."

"I wish mine had been able to tell me stories," Danthres said quietly. "She died getting me to Sorlin. I never really knew her."

"Mine died not long before I left Myverin," Torin added. "She was the one who got me interested in the world outside our walls."

Aleta added, "Mine died when I was a child—both my parents, in fact."

An awkward silence fell over the squadroom.

Then Dannee said, "My parents are in town for Maternal Day. I plan to bring them to the Dog and Duck. Why don't you all come with us? Manfred, Kellan, bring your mothers, too. And we can celebrate *all* our mothers, living and dead."

Danthres and Aleta said, "That's an awful idea" in perfect unison, while Torin said, "That is an excellent notion!"

With a wry look at Aleta, Danthres said, "If she thinks it's a bad idea, I should reconsider."

Aleta sighed. Danthres was also a halfbreed, elf and human, and she and Aleta had never gotten on.

Dannee then turned her pleading gaze onto Aleta. "Oh, please, Aleta? It will be wonderful!"

With a sigh, Aleta said, "Very well, but I think it's absurd. The Day of Mothers isn't for another month."

"Then we can do it again in a month," Dannee said.

Rolling her eyes and laughing, Aleta said, "Fine. I'll join you."

"Excellent!" Dannee clapped her hands. "We'll all gather at the Dog and Duck at nineteen tonight!"

A guard came in then saying there was a body on the docks in Mermaid Precinct. Manfred and Kellan were up next, so they went off to take the case, while everyone else settled down at their desks to do paperwork or whatever needed to be done.

Aleta thought about her mother and father, killed by the Elf Queen because of who they worshipped.

And she thought about Torin and Danthres, both inspired by their mothers, and Kellan and Manfred and Dannee, who had such wonderful memories of their mothers.

And she decided she would celebrate their lives with her squadmates. "Happy Maternal Day," she muttered.

Collegium Days

This is another vignette that provides some background on Torin, and also serves as a prequel to Wyvald ban Garin's appearance in Unicorn Precinct.

"THERE'S SOMEONE HERE TO SEE YOU."

Lieutenant Danthres Tresyllione said those words as Torin approached the portcullis that allowed him ingress to the castle. He was late for his shift, as usual, and a typical day would have Danthres already in the squadroom in the castle's eastern wing, eating the last of Sergeant Jonas's wife's pastries while mocking Torin for missing out on them again.

"To see me in particular?" Torin asked.

Danthres nodded. "Says his name is Mykal ban Dobsin."

Torin closed his eyes and let out a very long breath.

"Obviously, he's from Myverin," Danthres added. Torin's home, the distant, isolated city-state of Myverin was the only place in Flingaria that had the naming construction for men of "given name ban father's name." "Friend of yours?"

"Not exactly. He was one of the professors at the collegium when I attended."

TORIN BAN WYVALD RAISED HIS HAND, TO THE CHAGRIN OF PROFESSOR BAN Dobsin.

"Yes, ban Wyvald?" the professor said with a heavy sigh.

"What I don't understand is if the ideal form is unattainable, how can it possibly exist?"

"It's a theoretical construct, ban Wyvald. The point is that it is a thing to be aspired to."

"But if it doesn't exist, and cannot be attained, how can it be aspired to?"

"It is not always the goal that matters, ban Wyvald. It is the journey to that goal that —"

"No," Torin interrupted, *"I understand that, but if there's no hope of attaining the goal, what is the point?"*

WHEN TORIN ENTERED THE SQUADROOM, PROFESSOR BAN DOBSIN WAS standing next to Torin's desk, with two young people beside him. In the fifteen years since Torin had seen him last, the professor's hair had gone completely white.

"Professor!"

"Ban Wyvald!" Upon sighting Torin, ban Dobsin immediately walked toward him and gave Torin a massive hug.

Shocked by the embrace, it took Torin a moment to return it.

"It's so good to see you, ban Wyvald."

"Th-thank you, Professor, though I'm surprised to hear you say that, given our last conversation."

Breaking the embrace, ban Dobsin indicated the two people with him. "These are two of my students, Elyse val Nailyn and Alix ban Mallar. We're en route to Treemark for a symposium, and I had to stop by and see how my favorite student was doing."

"Favorite?" Torin shook his head. "If that's the case, Professor, you kept it quite the secret."

"YES, BAN WYVALD, WHAT CAN I DO FOR YOU?"

Torin very slowly walked into ban Dobsin's office. "I'm afraid I won't be attending class anymore, Professor."

"Why ever not? I confess, I will enjoy being able to get through a lecture without fifteen tiresome interruptions from you, but I'm surprised that the Chief Artisan's son will be permitted to withdraw from a class."

"I'm not just withdrawing from a class, I'm withdrawing from the collegium — and from Myverin. And it's against the wishes of the Chief Artisan."

"I would think so. I must say, ban Wyvald, I already thought of you as my worst student, but if you are willingly departing Myverin, then you're more than my worst student, you are the biggest fool in Flingaria."

Torin sighed. "I will miss our discussions, Professor. But it is one of the few things I will miss about this place."

"I wish I could say the same. Goodbye, ban Wyvald. If you survive more than a year outside Myverin's walls, it will be a small miracle."

"OH, NOW, I KNOW I WAS A BIT HARD ON YOU BACK THEN, BUT IT WAS ALL in service of stimulating your mind."

Torin decided it wouldn't be politic to point out that cruelty was rarely all that stimulating. "What is the symposium about?"

"Some elven philosophers have been living in exile in Treemark, and they're gathering some of the finest minds from all around Flingaria."

"I'm surprised that Shelli val Jaonne isn't going."

The professor winced. "I'm afraid Shelli died last year."

"Oh, I'm sorry." Torin had only met Shelli once or twice, but she was a brilliant mind, one of the finest philosophers in a city full of them.

And then he had to ask: "Wait, are you three the only people from Myverin attending?"

Nodding sadly, ban Dobsin said, "I'm afraid so. Nobody else was interested in leaving the safety of Myverin's walls."

"But you were?" Torin tried and failed to keep the shock out of his voice when he asked that question.

"Absolutely," ban Dobsin said emphatically. "And I have you to thank for it."

"Me?"

"Rumors of your adventures outside Myverin have trickled in over the years. And then when your father returned from his failed attempt to bring you home last year, we all learned about how you've thrived here. To some of us, it proved what we've believed all along—we are stagnating. You've been able to put your training to use here in Cliff's End. And I wish to go to the symposium to hear the thoughts and theories of people who have lived much less sheltered lives than we." Ban Dobsin put his hands on Torin's shoulders. "Thank you, ban Wyvald. You helped open my eyes to the rest of Flingaria. I'm hoping that our report from this symposium will convince more people."

"I hope it will too!" And Torin sincerely meant those words.

"HIGH MAGISTRATE, I UNDERSTAND THAT YOU'RE TRAVELLING TO CLIFF'S END *to retrieve your son."*

Wyvald ban Garin was mounting his horse and heading for the gates of Myverin when Professor ban Dobsin approached him. "Yes, I am."

"If I may ask – why?"

"It is his duty to assume the role of Chief Artisan."

"He abdicated that duty fifteen years ago, High Magistrate. You should appoint a new Chief Artisan and remain here and do your duty as High Magistrate."

"Do not presume to tell me how to raise my son, Professor."

"It is pointless to aspire to a goal you cannot achieve in reality." Ban Dobsin smiled. "It was, in fact, your son who taught me that."

"Your job was to teach my son, Professor. If he was teaching you, then I'd say you failed in your duty as a professor in the collegium."

Wyvald ban Garin then rode away from the city-state. Only when ban Dobsin knew he was out of earshot did he say, "And if he's been gone for fifteen years, then I'd say you failed in your duty as a father..."

Weekly Meeting

Finally, we have a prelude to the Dru-Doval breakfast meetings established here in Phoenix Precinct.

NO MATTER HOW MANY TIMES IT HAPPENED WITHOUT IT RESULTING IN ANY-thing bad, Captain Dru always took meetings with Lord Doval with a ton of trepidation.

It was a byproduct of secondhand evidence from the past. When Dru was a lieutenant, working as a detective in the Cliff's End Castle Guard, Captain Osric would occasionally be called to meet with Doval's late father, Lord Albin. Osric invariably returned from those meetings in a foul mood, which he would then take out on his subordinates.

However, when Dru thought about it, that trepidation was uncalled for. The situations were *not* analogous.

By the time Dru was promoted to lieutenant, Osric had been running the Castle Guard for Albin for the better part of a decade. The pair of them had built a certain trust, and Osric had earned a certain amount of autonomy.

Which meant, in real terms, that any time the lord of the demesne needed to talk to the captain of the Castle Guard, it was because of a problem. And problems that came from the western wing of the castle were almost always a *major* pain in the ass.

But Dru and Doval didn't have that lengthy a relationship, and both of them were also very much new to the job. Doval had inher-ited the job a year earlier from his brother Blayk—for his part, Blayk had only inherited the job from Albin a month previous, losing it only when it came out that Blayk engineered the poisoning of his father. And one of Doval's first orders when he took over was to promote Dru.

Besides which, Dru and Doval had actually developed a fairly friendly relationship. The pair of them had overseen a number of changes, including finally improving the quality of the Guard-issued swords, making the prison barge an official part of the Guard, now dubbed Manticore Precinct, the construction of a new neighborhood for refugees from Barlin following the fire there, and the creation of Phoenix Precinct to service "New Barlin," the unofficial name for that new neighborhood, which was officially Albinton after Doval's father.

"Ah, Captain, good to see you," Doval said, looking up from scribbling on a scroll as Dru entered.

"Uh, thanks, your lordship. Is everything all right?"

"Oh, tip-top. Yes, I'd say very tip-top indeed. I was looking at the reports from your people over the last month, and I'd say things are going swimmingly. Though I must say a few of the reports made very little sense to me. Have you had breakfast?"

Dru blinked. "Um, no." His wife Zan spent her days caring for assorted children of Cliff's End, and whatever breakfast she prepared was for the kids. Dru usually partook of Sergeant Jonas's wife's pastries when he reported for work, but the summons to this office had taken precedence over stuffing his face.

Clapping his hands and smiling the way he often did, Doval rose to his feet. "Excellent. Neither have I. Come with me, and we shall break our fast and you can explain some of the irregularities." He snatched some scrolls off his desk, and then led Dru to the Lord and Lady's Dining Room.

Dru had never set foot in the place, and had expected something more impressive than a tiny room with a window that provided a view of the Forest of Nimvale — one slightly different from the one in the Castle Guard squadroom on the other side of the castle — and one table with two chairs.

Over the course of wheatcakes, sausage in gravy, and tea, Dru explained some of the anomalies — most of which were the result of either Arn Kellan's poor descriptive skills, Dannee Ocly's flowery style of reporting, or Danthres Tresyllione's wretched handwriting.

"This has been very enlightening, Captain. And I see that the rate at which crimes have been committed seems to have levelled off."

"Somewhat," Dru said after swallowing a bite of sausage. "Thefts and murders are down, but assaults are up, especially in Goblin and Mermaid. And I think the honeymoon period with Phoenix is starting to come down, and crime's gonna go up now that everyone's used to there being more Guards around."

Just as Dru finished his sentence, the time-chimes rang out eight times. "Interesting. I'd love to hear more about that, but I have a meeting at half-eight that I must go prepare for. But we should do this again."

"We should?" Dru asked the question before he could stop himself, and hoped that his lordship didn't notice the dread undertone in his voice as he made the query.

"Absolutely." Doval got to his feet. "Let us do this on the morning of the final day of every week. It will give us a chance to go over what has happened in the past seven days and prepare for the next seven."

"I—" Dru had about two dozen objections, precisely none of which he could possibly voice to the person who was pretty much in charge of the entire city-state. So instead, he rather weakly finished: "—would love that."

Clapping his hands once, he grinned. "Excellent! See you next week, then!"

With that, Doval departed at a brisk pace.

Dru finished off his sausage, gulped down his now-lukewarm tea, and then walked more leisurely to the eastern wing of the castle. *Now I'm starting to understand why Osric always got so cranky...*

ABOUT THE AUTHOR

Keith R.A. DeCandido is a white male in his early fifties, approximately two hundred pounds. He was last seen in the wilds of the Bronx, New York City, though he is often sighted in other locales. Usually, he is armed with a laptop computer, which some have classified as a deadly weapon. Through use of this laptop, he has inflicted sixty novels, as well as an indeterminate number of comic books, nonfiction, novellas, and works of short fiction on an unsuspecting reading public. Many of these are set in the milieus of television shows, games, movies, and comic books, among them *Star Trek, Alien, Cars, Resident Evil, Doctor Who, Supernatural, World of Warcraft*, Marvel Comics, and many more.

We have received information confirming that more stories involving Danthres, Torin, and the city-state of Cliff's End can be found in the novels *Dragon Precinct, Unicorn Precinct, Goblin Precinct, Gryphon Precinct, Mermaid Precinct, Tales from Dragon Precinct*, and the forthcoming *Manticore Precinct* and *More Tales from Dragon Precinct*.

His other recent crimes against humanity include an urban fantasy series taking place in DeCandido's native Bronx (*A Furnace Sealed* and the forthcoming *Feat of Clay*, with more threatened); the urban fantasy short story collection *Ragnarok and a Hard Place: More Tales of Cassie Zukav, Weirdness Magnet*; the *Systema Paradoxa* novella *All-the-Way House*; the graphic novel prequel to the *Resident Evil: Infinite Darkness* TV series, *The Beginning*; short stories in the anthologies *Devilish & Divine, Three Time Travelers Walk Into…, The Fans are Buried Tales*, and in the *Phenomenons* and *Thrilling Adventure Yarns* series; and nonfiction about pop culture for Tor.com, the *Subterranean Blue Grotto, Outside In*, and *Gold Archive* series, and on his own Patreon. Among his known associates are collaborators in his crimes against humanity: Dr. Munish K. Batra (the serial-killer thriller *Animal*), David Sherman (the military SF novel *To Hell and Regroup*), and Gregory A. Wilson (the award-winning graphic novel *Icarus*).

If you see DeCandido, do not approach him, but call for backup immediately. He is often seen in the company of a suspicious-looking woman who goes by the street name of "Wrenn," as well as several as-yet-unidentified cats. A full dossier can be found at DeCandido.net

PATRONS OF CLIFF'S END

Adam Nemo
Amanda Nixon
Andrea Hunter
Andrew Kaplan
Andy Hunter
Anonymous Reader
Aramanth Dawe
Austin Hoffey
Aven Lumi
Aysha Rehm
Bea Hersh-Tudor
Becky B
Benjamin Adler
Bess Turner
Bethany Tomerlin Prince
Betsy Cameron
Bill Kohn
Bill Schulz & family
Brad Jurn
Brendan Coffey
Brendan Lonehawk
Brian G
Brian Quirt
Brooks Moses
Carol Gyzander
Carol J. Guess
Carol Jones
Caroline Westra
Carolyn and Stephen Stein
Carolyn Rowland

Cathy Green
Chad Bowden
Charles Barouch
Charles Deal
Chris Bauer, novelist, Blessid
Trauma series
Christopher J. Burke
Christopher Weuve
Cori Paige
Craig "Stevo" Stephenson
Cristov Russell
Dale A Russell
Dan Persons
Daniel Korn
Danielle Ackley-McPhail
Danny Chamberlin
Darke Conteur
Darrell Z. Grizzle
David Goldstein
David Lee Summers
David Medinnus
Debra L. Lieven
Denise and Raphael Sutton
Dennis P Campbell
Diana Botsford
Donna M. Hogg
Dr. Kat Crispin
Edwin Purcell
Ef Deal
Elaine Tindill-Rohr

Ellery Rhodes
Elyse M Grasso
Emily Rebecca Weed Baisch
Eric Slaney
Erin A.
Fantasy Supporter
Gary Phillips
Gav I.
Glori Medina
GraceAnne Andreassi
    DeCandido
Greg Levick
Heidi Pilewski
Hollie Buchanan
IAMTW
Isaac 'Will It Work' Dansicker
J. Linder
Jacen Leonard
Jack Deal
Jack Deal
James Hallam
James Johnston
Jason R Burns
Jeffrey Harlan
Jennifer L. Pierce
Jeremy Bottroff
Jim Gotaas
jjmcgaffey
John Keegan
John L. French
John Markley
John Peters
John Schoffstall
Jonathan Haar
Josh Ward
Jp
Judith Waidlich
Jules
Julian White
Julie Strange
Kal Powell

Karen Krah
Kate Myers
Katherine Hempel
Katie
Kay Hafner
Kelly Pierce
Kelsey M
Kerry aka Trouble
Kimberly Catlett
Kit Kindred
krinsky
KT Magrowski
Lark Cunningham
Lawrence M. Schoen
LCW Allingham
Lee Jamilkowski
Linda Pierce
Lisa Kruse
Lisa Venezia
Lori & Maurice Forrester
Lorraine J. Anderson
Lowell Gilbert
maileguy
Maree Pavletich
Marilyn B
Mark Bergin
Mark Newman
Mark Squire
Mary Perez
Matthew Barr
Maureen Lewis
Mauria Reich
Megan Murphy Davis
Melanie Ball
Michael A. Burstein
Michael Brooker
Mikaela Irish
Mike "PsychoticDreamer"
    Bentley
Mike Bunch
Mike Crate

Mike Zipser
Mina Ellyse
Miriam Seidel
Nathan Turner
Nathaniel Adams
Nicholas Ahlhelm
Pat Knuth
Patrick Purcell
Paul Ryan
Paul van Oven
Pepita Hogg-Sonnenberg
Peter D Engebos
pjk
Pookster
prophet
Raphael Bressel
RAW
Rich Gonzalez
Richard Novak
Richard O'Shea
River
Rob Menaul
Robert Claney
Rochelle
Rose Caratozzolo
Ross Hathaway
Ruthenia
Sally Wiener Grotta

Saul Jaffe
Scantrontb
Scott Elson
Scott Thede
Sheryl R. Hayes
Sidney Whitaker
Steph Parker
Stephanie Lucas
Stephen Ballentine
Stephen Cheng
Stephen Lesnik
Stephen Rubin
Steve Locke
Steven Purcell
Stuart Chaplin
Svend Andersen
The Creative Fund
The Reckless Pantalones
Tim DuBois
Tina M Noe Good
Todd Dashoff
Tom B.
ToniAnn & Kyle
Tracy 'Rayhne' Fretwell
Ty Drago
Vee Luvian
Will "scifantasy" Frank
William J. Donahue